"Do you still tread on toes?"

Melinda asked flippantly.

"I might have crippled valley girls at barn dances in my teens," Kyle admitted, "but I'm more proficient now." He drew her into his arms. "I still prefer the old-fashioned way, don't you?"

Melinda wasn't sure that she did. She was all too aware of his warm fingers entwined with hers, the firmness of his broad palm spread across the small of her back and the tangy scent of his after-shave.

"Your hand is cold," he said suddenly, chafing her fingers.

"I hadn't noticed." It must be the tension, she thought.

"Cold hands, warm heart, they say." Were the dark eyes teasing, or serious?

He pulled her closer and a small shiver ran through her. Kyle's hand slid farther around her waist, drawing her closer until her breasts and thighs were brushing against him. They swayed gently to the rhythm of a blues number. If she closed her eyes, it was just like old times....

Dear Reader,

Summer romance . . . does anything tug at the heartstrings more? We've all experienced poignant first love at a vacation resort or those balmy summer nights on the porch swing with that special man—if not in real life, then certainly in the pages of Silhouette Romance novels, the perfect summertime reading!

This month, our heroines find their heroes around the world—in Mexico, Italy, Australia—*and* right in their own backyard. And what heroes they find, from the mysterious stranger to the charming man of their dreams!

July continues our WRITTEN IN THE STARS series. Each month in 1991, we're proud to present a book that focuses on the hero—and his astrological sign. July features the passionate, possessive and vulnerable Cancerian man in Val Whisenand's *For Eternity*.

Silhouette Romance novels *always* reflect the magic of love in heartwarming stories that will make you laugh and cry and move you time and time again. In the months to come, watch for books by your all-time favorites, including Diana Palmer, Brittany Young, Annette Broadrick and many others.

I hope you enjoy this book and all our future Silhouette Romance stories. We'd love to hear from you!

Sincerely,

Valerie Susan Hayward
Senior Editor

FRANCES LLOYD

Let Me Call You Sweetheart

Silhouette Romance

Published by Silhouette Books New York

America's Publisher of Contemporary Romance

SILHOUETTE BOOKS
300 E. 42nd St., New York, N.Y. 10017

LET ME CALL YOU SWEETHEART

ISBN: 0-373-08804-3

First Silhouette Books printing July 1991

Printed in the U.S.A.

Books by Frances Lloyd

Silhouette Romance

Savage Moon #200
Desert Rose #319
Wild Horizons #425
The Castaways #473
Tomorrow's Dawn #497
Touched by Magic #549
The Takeover Man #569
Lord of the Glen #624
Let Me Call You Sweetheart #804

FRANCES LLOYD

lives in Melbourne, Australia. Although many of her books have Australian settings and vividly reflect her love of the outback, she and her husband also like to travel overseas researching romantic backgrounds. When she can spare time from writing, she is a keen bird observer and gardener.

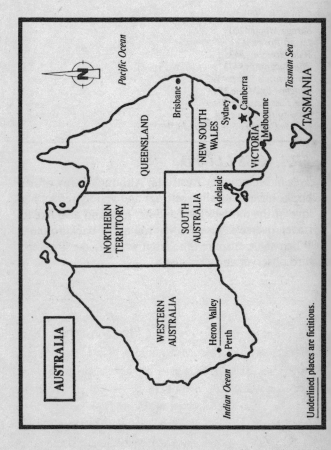

AUSTRALIA

Pacific Ocean

Tasman Sea

TASMANIA

Brisbane

QUEENSLAND

NEW SOUTH WALES

Canberra

Sydney

VICTORIA

Melbourne

Adelaide

NORTHERN TERRITORY

SOUTH AUSTRALIA

WESTERN AUSTRALIA

Heron Valley

Perth

Indian Ocean

Underlined places are fictitious.

Chapter One

Melinda absentmindedly squeezed too much detergent into the sink and when she turned the tap on, it frothed up excessively. She slapped the froth down.

"Oh, I wish Kyle hadn't come back!"

Melinda clenched her teeth on the impulsive words and raked a damp hand through her unruly red-gold hair. What on earth had made her say that? She hadn't even been thinking about him—had she? She swiped again at the fizzing mountain of froth as though it were his fault, and a cluster of bubbles floated around the kitchen. They caught the rays of the just-risen sun and reflected rainbowed windows. The beauty of the little colored reflections released her tension and she smiled. What was the matter with her? There was no reason on earth to be uptight about Kyle. He'd hurt her once, but he couldn't hurt her now.

She gazed past the bubbles out the window, across the yard to the wide vista of the vineyard beyond. The long rows of newly shooting vines were pale green ribbons against the rich, red loam. They stretched in a vanishing perspective toward the low hills that enclosed Heron Valley with a haze of indigo. Although it was still very early, she could hear a tractor droning in the distance, and magpies were warbling in the big red gum next to the house. It was the time of day Melinda loved best, when the whole world was waking up, when it was possible to imagine that the valley *was* the whole world.

She sighed deeply, her gray eyes softening. She loved the valley, and yet lately she had been experiencing bouts of restlessness, had even felt that something indefinable was missing from her life. Of course it was usual to feel a bit that way at reunion time. Her best friends from high school, who had all gone away while she had stayed behind and taken over her father's vineyard, would be coming next week for the biennial get-together. As she dried the dishes Melinda glanced at the postcards pinned to the kitchen notice board. There would be only four of them this time: Katherine, Sylvana, Rose and herself.

The sound of barking at the back door reminded her that Polly, her father's old kelpie, wanted her walk, so she hung up the dish towel, calling to the impatient dog that she was coming. With Polly jogging along just ahead, Melinda took her usual route down through the vines to Jarrahwood, the swath of bush that divided her property, Riversham, from the Macintosh place, Heronvale.

When she came up to the ramshackle old hut by the creek she paused, suddenly remembering with uncomfortable clarity that it had been in the hut amid the cobwebs and dust that Kyle Macintosh had first kissed her. Melinda hurried past the now-derelict building, and at the creek crossing she paused again. The stream was running faster than she'd expected and water covered the stepping-stones. She would have to take her sneakers off to cross.

As she sat on a fallen log to undo the laces, the sound of a dog barking made her glance up. Rufus, the Heronvale collie, was bounding down the opposite bank of the creek. Polly answered him joyfully, tail wagging.

Behind the dog came Kyle. Funny how he still favored checked shirts, Melinda mused, and gumboots with his jeans tucked into the tops. He waded easily across the full creek. He was a large man, tall with muscular arms and legs and a broad chest. Dark eyes dominated a granitelike face framed by a lot of dark wavy hair, and his olive skin always looked tanned, summer or winter. His expression was somber until he spotted her.

"Hello, Melly. What are you doing here?"

She put on a young voice and mock rebelliousness. "Playing truant!" Since he'd come back to the valley, for some reason she found herself constantly being flippant when she spoke to him.

He sat beside her, large hands spread on his knees, a touch of humor in his eyes. "Those were the days!" He gave an exaggerated sigh, but Melinda knew he didn't hanker for school days. He hadn't been able to wait to get away from the valley.

He smiled. She'd always been melted by that smile, half teasing, half challenging. And his eyes, dark as ripe olives, still seemed to convey a special intimacy. His presence was powerful, very masculine. He seemed to fill a space larger than he was. Melinda wondered what he was remembering.

"School days were fun," she said, "but I guess we'd both still settle for the present and future, given the choice."

His gaze sharpened. "How do you see your future, Melly?" he asked, as though he really was interested.

She shrugged. "More of the same, I suppose. Planting vines, picking the grapes, crushing, fermenting, bottling...." She laughed, but the sound was peculiarly hollow and her voice shook a little as she added, "I go with the seasons, Kyle. I pray there won't be rain when the grapes are set and ready to pick, or floods when we're trying to prune, and drought when we need rain."

"Are you happy?" The question was as sharp as a poke with a stick.

Melinda was startled. He had not questioned her so intimately before. "Happy? Of course I am," she answered. "I'm too busy to be otherwise. I love my work. My life's very satisfying." It was hard at that moment, though, to shut out the memory of how unhappy she'd been ten years ago after they'd quarreled and he'd left the valley. It had been her decision not to go with him, but she'd been hurt when only months later she'd learned of his marriage to an actress.

"I expected you'd be married with a tribe of kids by now," he said with a quizzical lifting of dark eyebrows.

Melinda said airily, "Oh, I nearly tied the knot a couple of times, but—" she shrugged again "—it didn't work out."

"Because you wouldn't leave the valley?" His lips thinned and past reproach still echoed in his voice.

Their eyes clashed. It was the first time he had referred even obliquely to her refusal to go with him when he'd left ten years before. Melinda said tautly, "It's not a crime, surely, to be happy to stay in the place where you were born? The world might be in an even worse mess than it is if everyone went haring off and nobody stayed put."

He chuckled and patted her shoulder as a kind of apology. "You might have a point there, Melly. I guess it does take all sorts."

Melinda drew circles in the dirt with a stick, not looking at him. She didn't care that he derided her. She knew she had made the right decision. Hadn't she?

Kyle went on, "You know, what I like about Heron Valley is that it never changes. Neither the landscape nor the people."

"I thought that was what you hated about it," Melinda said with irony. "I thought that was what you wanted to escape."

"Sure I did. And I haven't suddenly become sentimental. But the valley intrigues me. People don't even seem to get any older. You look just the same, Melly." He studied her face intently.

She broke her stick into small pieces. "Look hard enough and you'll discover a few lines."

He was shaking his head as he peered more closely at her, smiling. "Only laughter lines. You really haven't changed at all." His face was close to hers and warm male breath fanned her cheek. Awareness sprang like an electric arc from man to woman and then Kyle drew back as though recoiling from a shock while Melinda stared into his startled eyes, nonplussed. She stood up hastily, then abruptly sat down again to untie her shoes.

"Going paddling?" he asked with a grin, "or fishing for gilgies?"

Memories of hunting the small freshwater crayfish with Kyle swamped Melinda for a moment. "We never caught many, did we?" She laughed. "I've given up those childish pursuits, Kyle. I just want to cross the creek because Polly likes to go this way for her walk. If I don't take my shoes off I'll get them wet."

"No, you won't," he said, getting up, and before she realized what he intended he had scooped her up and was carrying her across.

"Put me down!" she shrieked, but her struggles only made him tighten his grip.

He paused, lifting an eyebrow at her outrage. "In the water?"

"No, you fool! Kyle, let me go...." Chagrined laughter was choking her. Kyle had always been one for horseplay and she had often been his victim.

When they reached the other side he set her down and then, fastening his arms securely around her slim body, clamped her to him so tightly she expected to hear her ribs crack. The look that passed between them was pure primitive communication. With shock, Melinda realized that the embers of an old fire were not quite dead, and far too easily fanned into leaping flames.

"Thanks for the lift." Her voice was a ragged whisper and butterflies were having a ball in her stomach. She was furious with herself.

"You're welcome," he answered slowly, the husky timbre of his voice betraying that emotion had been on the brink of getting out of hand. Melinda called her dog. "Polly! Come on, old girl, let's go and say hello to Mrs. Marchant." To Kyle she added, "Mrs. Marchant always has a bone for her."

He said, "I'll walk part way with you."

They trudged through the bush along little-used but still-visible tracks, saying little. They were scrambling over a fallen tree when a gleam of pale yellow caught Melinda's eye and she paused, bending to look at the clump of orchids growing near the tangled roots now exposed.

"Look, Kyle. Cowslips. They're the first I've seen this spring." Glowing with pleasure in the discovery, she glanced up at him.

"No, you haven't changed," he mused, resting his arm across her shoulders as he squatted beside her. "You used to draw and paint wildflowers exquisitely. Do you still paint?"

Melinda looked at him over her shoulder, surprised. "You remember that?" A warm trembling inside her that had no business being there was starting up again. "Yes, I do, when I've time. I've been thinking of using wildflowers on my new wine labels. Watercolors. What do you think?"

Feeling they were too close, she stood up, but before she could widen the space between them Kyle caught hold of her hand. "I think that's a splendid idea. Especially using your own paintings. Wine labels signed by the wine maker! They'll become collectors' items.''

She flicked a tangle of red-gold hair off her forehead and pulled her hand away. "You're mocking me."

The lines between his eyes deepened. "No, Melly. I'm wondering, though, if you ever regret staying in the valley, puttering about in a vineyard, designing the odd wine label hardly anybody will ever see, when you could have had a career, developed your artistic talent, made something of yourself instead of wasting your life in this backwater."

Melinda flinched at what was an echo of past tirades, but refused to let him goad her. "I do not putter. I work extremely hard to keep the vineyard going. It's a very satisfying occupation, Kyle. I don't think I'm wasting my life."

He stood up. "You always did have a mind of your own, Melly." Then a smile appeared. "Sorry! I didn't mean to berate you. You chose to stay in the valley and that's your business."

"What you mean is, I made my bed so I'm obliged to lie in it. Well, I find it a very comfortable bed."

With sudden vehemence and a searching look he grasped her shoulders. "No regrets at all?"

"None." Except that deep inside her lurked a treacherous longing to feel his arms around her tightly....

"Sure?"

She shrugged away from him. What on earth was the matter with her today? One minute she was arguing with him, the next wanting to fall into his arms.

Kyle took her face in his hands, lightly turning it from side to side, examining her profile, and murmured, "Wildflowers are often quite small and inconspicuous, but they have a hidden beauty for those who care to look closely. You have much in common with wildflowers, Melly."

His eyes were too close, too compelling. Melinda twisted out of his grasp and fixed her gaze on the clump of orchids gleaming palely in the dappled sunlight, almost camouflaged by it. She tried to concentrate on the delicate pointed petals, the open lips at the center of each flower, but it was her own lips that opened against Kyle's mouth. Only for a moment. Cheeks burning, she summoned enough strength to drag herself away. "Kyle—*that* was going a bit far."

Turning her back on him, she called again to Polly and without another word set off along the track. Kyle caught up with her and they walked on in silence until they came to the rise from where both the Marchant house and Heronvale homestead could be seen.

"I'll leave you here," Kyle said.

"Yes. See you." Melinda wanted to get away, yet found it hard to tear herself away from him.

"Melly..."

She stopped and looked back. "Yes?"

"I'm sorry if I offended you."

She ran her tongue over her lips and forced out her answer. "That's all right, Kyle." Only when she was out of his sight did she brush the sudden tears out of her eyes. Stupid idiot! she castigated herself. The last thing she must do was go all soft on Kyle Macintosh once more. He'd be gone again before she could blink. And he wasn't likely to ask her to go with him this time. Not that she'd go if he did. She regretted nothing.

Melinda found Mrs. Marchant near her front gate, talking to a couple of men. Beside them was a large board, buttressed by stout supports. The board was facing the road, away from her, but Melinda's breath caught painfully in her chest. Jarrahwood must be up for sale. She couldn't believe it. For a moment or two she just stood transfixed, muttering "No!" vehemently to herself. The men moved away and threw their tools into their truck. As they drove off Mrs. Marchant turned around, saw Melinda and waved.

"Hello, Melly."

Melinda joined her and they stood reading the skillfully printed real estate agent's board in stunned silence.

"For sale by auction." Melly's lips formed the words soundlessly. "One hundred acres and comfortable three-bedroom timber cottage with five acres of vines and orchard, and two poultry sheds and runs. River frontage, and creek through property. Ample water. Great development potential for vines, orchard, market garden or pasture...."

Melinda turned to the old lady. "You're selling," she said incredulously. She couldn't help the note of accusation. It was such a shock. Jarrahwood had belonged to Marchants for generations.

Lips pursed, Mrs. Marchant said in a quavering voice, "I was just going in to make some tea. You'll stop and have a cup with me, Melly?"

Melinda walked back to the house with her. Mrs. Marchant didn't mention the auction until she had put the kettle on. Melinda waited, sensing that the old woman was as choked as she was. Finally she said, "Why?"

"The old place is getting a bit run-down. I can't do as much as I used to since my legs started playing me up. Sam says it's too much for me now and I suppose he's right. He wants me to go into a retirement village."

"Would you like that?"

Mrs. Marchant's face revealed her reluctance, but she said slowly and resignedly, "I suppose I'll have to. Can't stay here and let the place fall down around my ears, can I?"

Sam talking, thought Melinda. "It wouldn't if those sons of yours did a bit of renovating for you. You're still able to look after yourself and probably will be able to for a few more years yet. If you don't want to go..."

"I don't!" said Mrs. Marchant with feeling, and Melinda didn't miss the sudden brightness of tears in her eyes, or the surreptitious wiping away of them. "I've lived here more than fifty years."

"Well, nobody can make you go," said Melinda, sparking. "You don't have to just because Sam—"

"Sam needs capital to expand his electronics business and unless I sell up..." Mrs. Marchant looked quite guilty about her reluctance. "The boys aren't interested in Jarrahwood, Melly. It's a valuable piece of real estate, they say, because it's the only undeveloped acreage left in the valley. It's bound to fetch a good price, and they might as well have the money now as have to wait until I'm dead."

Melinda didn't know what to say. She was shattered by the news.

Mrs. Marchant changed the subject. "I wonder how much longer young Kyle Macintosh will be staying at Heronvale. It's a shame he's divorced. The little boy seems a bright lad."

But Melinda was not listening. She was hearing in her head the ominous grind of bulldozers as they tore down her precious bushland. "I'd better be going," she said, almost choking on the lump in her throat. "Thanks for the tea."

As she walked home the stark reality of Jarrahwood's being sold and probably cleared was seeping deeper and deeper into her mind. She suddenly felt quite sick with dismay. What could she do to save it?

The morning was more than half gone, but Melinda settled down in her office to try to catch up on some paperwork before lunch. She was not very successful. Anguish over Jarrahwood kept intruding. Was it immature to feel sentimental about a few acres of bush? Kyle would think so. Shouldn't she just accept change and call it progress, too? Was she still living too much in the past, and foolish to expect life to continue serenely in the same pattern forever?

Presently Melinda made herself a snack, ate it quickly and then returned to the office. She still couldn't concentrate properly and was glad of the temporary reprieve when she saw Rocky striding across the yard toward the house. With him were his own son, Robert, and Matthew, Kyle's son. At their heels galloped Rufus with old Polly bringing up the

rear more sedately. Melinda met them at the back
door.

"Matt's come over to give us a hand with fixing the
overhead trellis," Rocky said. "Okay?" He winked at
Melinda.

"Does your father know you're here, Matt?" Melinda asked.

Matthew nodded. His dark eyes were exactly like
Kyle's, with that secretive closed look, so you never
knew what he was thinking. She was glad that the two
boys, being the same age, had quickly become friends.

A car horn drew their attention to the bottom of the
driveway where the mail van was just pulling away
from the mailbox on the gatepost.

"We'll get it!" cried Matthew.

"Race you!" challenged Robert, and the boys ran
off with Rufus in hot pursuit.

"Great kid," said Rocky. "Needs a mother, though,
and some brothers and sisters."

"Kyle will probably marry again soon." She
sounded stiff.

Rocky shot her a quizzical look. "Matt's mighty
fond of you, Mel, and isn't it about time you settled
down? It's no life for a young woman living alone and
devoting herself to vines."

Melinda colored. "Really, Rocky!"

He grinned. "You like him, don't you?"

"Matthew? Yes, of course I do. He's a great kid."

"I meant Kyle."

"Rocky," said Melinda sternly, "stop romancing.
Kyle and I are like chalk and cheese. Besides, he's not
interested in valley girls. He moves in a different world

now. He likes his women to have a bit of sophistication.''

''I bet he prefers 'em warm and tender, though, as much as any man,'' said Rocky, enjoying the discomfort of his young, gray-eyed, redheaded and very attractive employer. He and his wife, Debra, had tried matchmaking many times, but Melinda had always slipped out of the net, even on the most promising occasions. It was very frustrating.

Matthew, breathless, ran up and thrust the bundle into Melinda's hands, grinning. ''Looks like masses of bills, Melly.''

Melinda grimaced. ''What else? Bills and catalogs. We never get exciting mail.''

But today there was an exciting letter in the bundle, which she did not see until Rocky and the boys had left her. Back in her office, she flung the mail onto her desk. The force snapped the rubber band holding the items together, and as the envelopes fanned out the logo in the top left-hand corner of one caught her eye. Instantly she grabbed it, holding her breath as, with trembling fingers, she slit it open and withdrew the letter.

''I don't believe it!'' she whispered as she scanned the page. ''I just don't believe it....'' Her mouth quivered, her nose wrinkled and there was a feeling like champagne bubbles in her blood. She read the letter twice, then gave a shout of exultation. She was beginning to believe it now.

''Wait till Kyle hears about this!'' she exclaimed. ''Puttering, indeed. How dare he!''

With the letter fluttering in her hand she raced out the back door and sped across the yard and down the

hill to the winery where she knew Gianni was working. Gianni Ricchioni, her father's old wine maker,
must be the first to hear the sensational news. She
burst into the fermentation room calling, "Gianni!
Where are you?" Her shout reverberated off the
shining stainless steel tanks, but there was no reply.
Melinda raced into the bottling room.

"Gianni . . . Oh, there you are."

"What's the matter?" He came toward her, his
gnarled face anxious. "What's wrong?"

"What's wrong?" she echoed. "Nothing, Gianni.
It's what's right!" She waved the letter under his nose.
"We've done it!" Her eyes were alight with excite-
ment.

"What have we done? Nothing illegal, I hope."

"Read this." She shoved the letter at him, but he
declined.

"Read it to me. I haven't got my reading glasses."

"All right, but hang on to your hat, Gianni. This is
going to knock you for six." Laughter bubbled up.
"And you and a few other people are going to have to
eat your hats."

"You have won the lottery," Gianni said in amazement.

"Better than that," said Melinda. "Listen." She
read aloud the words that had made her want to turn
cartwheels. She rushed through the preliminaries and
then with emphasis, intoned, "Winner of a gold medal
at the Sydney show...." Melinda savored those words
reverently, and in a tone of barely suppressed excitement continued with the judges' citation. "A new light
red reminiscent of the Rhône wines of France, with a
bouquet faintly redolent of wildflowers on a misty

spring morning, an intriguing fruity flavor and a crisp finish that lingers nostalgically on the palate...."

The words came out in such a rush she had to stop, breathless. Her expressive features broke into a smile of triumph. "Gianni, we've done it! We've won a gold medal!" The letter floated to the floor as she grabbed the elderly wine maker and whirled him around in a victory pirouette, the waves of gleaming red-gold hair tumbling across her forehead, her eyes shining.

Huffing and puffing and grinning under his drooping gray mustache, he said, "Congratulations! *Molto bene! Bravissimo!*" and kissed her on both cheeks enthusiastically. "You have made my day!"

Melinda kissed him back and they hugged each other gleefully. "Oh, Gianni, I'm so thrilled, so excited!" she exclaimed, stooping to retrieve the precious letter. "It's what we've toiled for all these years." Her smile slipped a little and she became wistful. "I only wish Dad..."

"He would be very proud," said Gianni, "to see his daughter following in his footsteps." Face deadpan, he added, "You will be a very good wine maker one day, *bambina.*"

Melinda laughed. Trust Gianni to cut her down to size. One gold medal didn't make an expert. "I ought to be, with you and Dad as my mentors," she said. "It's really your triumph, Gianni."

He was generous. "No, no. This is your success. You nurtured the vines and decided when to harvest, you selected the vintages, you did the blending...no, no, it is yours, Melinda, all yours."

Melinda read the letter again. Her eyes misted over as she thought of her father and how hard he had worked to achieve his dream of producing champion-class wines with the Riversham label. He had died before his dream was realized, but she knew he would not begrudge her any success she might build on the foundations he had laid. If she'd needed any reassurance that she'd been right to stay in the valley, this was it.

"Gold medal," she murmured, still hardly able to believe it. On her way out she pirouetted again from sheer exuberance. Too late to prevent it as she whirled through the doorway, her nose collided with the breastbone of the man who was just entering.

"Steady on—where's the fire?" Smiling dark brown eyes sent her emotions into turmoil for the second time that day as Kyle Macintosh looked down from his six-foot height at her five foot three with laconic amusement while his strong arms steadied her. She hadn't expected to see him again so soon and his sudden appearance scooped out a trembling hollow inside her.

"Hello, Kyle," she said, shrugging herself out of his grasp. She dived through the door and started to march toward the house, handing him the letter casually. "How about this?" She couldn't keep the triumph out of her voice. "Not bad for a putterer, is it?"

Matching his stride easily to hers, he read, and as they paused at the kitchen door he laid a large hand on her shoulder and pulled her around to face him. He smiled broadly and was generous. "This is great news, Mel. No wonder you're all lit up like a Christmas tree! Congratulations. It's a real feather in your cap. And well deserved. I'm sure there's loud applause up yonder." Smiling, he jerked his chin skyward and, exerting a slight pressure on her shoulder, added softly, "Bram would be very proud."

The excitement, his respectful tone as he mentioned her father, together with the conflict of emotions already seething in her, were too much and Melinda cracked. As though a bung had been released from a barrel, tears flowed down her cheeks and she couldn't stop them. She was hardly aware of Kyle's hand drawing her toward him or his arms enfolding her until she felt her cheek resting against the softness of his flannelette shirt, which she proceeded to dampen thoroughly in a shameless and uninhibited display of emotion.

Regaining control with an effort, she pulled back, embarrassed. "Sorry. . . ."

"You miss him, don't you?" Kyle said quietly.

Choked, she nodded. "It's not fair. He worked so hard to make a name for our wine, and now I'll get the benefit . . . all the kudos if we're successful."

He pushed open the screen door and they went through the small, cluttered vestibule of the old homestead into the kitchen. Kyle pushed her into a chair at the table. "You need a cup of tea."

Melinda didn't protest. It had never been much use protesting when Kyle made up his mind to do something, because he would do it anyway. She supposed his often-autocratic manner came from his Italian mother, whose family had been aristocratic back in Calabria.

Melinda leaned her elbows on the table, propped her chin on her linked fingers and watched him fill the electric kettle, rattle cups onto saucers and spoon tea from the old willow-pattern caddy into the brown china teapot. She marveled at how homely such a so-phisticated man could be. He hadn't been in the Riv-ersham kitchen for years, yet he seemed perfectly at home there.

"Rosa told me Matthew was over here again," said Kyle.

"He's down on the flats with Rocky and Robert fixing the trellis. I think he's learning to speak Serbo-Croatian as well as wield the wire strainers." She chuckled. "He's a quick learner, your son, so Rocky tells me. He insists he wants to be a vigneron!" Not a hotelier like his father. Matthew was very positive about that. Melinda wondered if Kyle hoped his son would follow in his footsteps and take over the string of small, classy hotels he owned around Australia. Or didn't he mind what career his son chose? Melinda often puzzled over Kyle's attitude toward Matt. He seemed so stiff with the boy. And she worried that Matt's preference for messing about down at Rivers-ham instead of up at Heronvale was only partly be-cause of Robert—that he also wanted to escape from his father.

Kyle leaned against the kitchen counter, arms folded across his broad chest. "You must tell me if he's a nuisance."

"Nuisance?" She laughed. "I've told you before, he's as good as gold, Kyle. It's good for him to have Robert to play with. Rocky keeps an eye on them and those kids really do help, you know. They wrote out all the labels for my samples the other day. I daresay he'd be more eager to help around the place at Heronvale if he had a playmate there. You don't mind him com-ing down here, do you?"

"No, of course not." Having poured tea into the cups, he pushed hers across the table. Melinda felt uneasy because of their encounter that morning.

"I daresay he's deliberately forgotten he has a dentist's appointment this afternoon."

Melinda grimaced. "Do you blame him?"

For a few minutes they talked about the gold medal and what it might mean to Riversham's future fortunes.

"Orders are bound to start rolling in," Kyle predicted. "I'd better put one in right away for my cellars."

Melinda's eyes widened. "You mean you'll put it on your hotels' wine list?"

"Why not? It's a very good wine. I was going to do that anyway."

Melinda was overcome. "That's terrific of you, Kyle, but you don't have to—"

"I know, and believe me, I don't invest in plonk even if it is made by an old friend. I buy the best." He gave her a straight look. "I was only teasing about the puttering."

Melinda sighed. "Oh, Kyle, I really feel I've *arrived* at last."

Kyle drained his teacup. "I'd better collect Matthew."

But he didn't move at once and there was a slightly painful pause. Finally Melly clattered her empty cup onto its saucer, rose and pulled her T-shirt down, unconsciously stretching the material over her shapely curves as she allowed her hands to rest on her hips. "Thank you for making the tea, Kyle. I'm all right now. Thinking about Dad still makes me rather emotional.'' How gauche he must think her. To him she must seem a rather naive young girl still, not a twenty-nine-year-old woman. Kissing her this morning had just been a tease.

Her stance drew the T-shirt tautly across her small, firm breasts and emphasized her narrow waist. Kyle took a long, leisurely look, eyes drifting slowly down past her slim hips and smooth, flat pelvis, admiring her shapely legs in tight stretch jeans. She was still as tantalizing a ball of energy and fire as ever, a perennial tomboy in a very feminine guise. It was tempting to think of her as still a fresh and innocent young girl, but there were subtle changes that belied that impression. The male in him wondered about her innocence; the entrepreneur admired the way she ran Riversham.

He rose, too, and Melinda suddenly felt sympathy for him. A messy divorce, a bitter custody battle and his father's death coming one after the other had taken their toll. There were lines of grief and anxiety still etched around his mouth and eyes.

He looked seriously into her face for a moment, then lifted both hands and with his forefingers traced the shape of a smile from the corners of her mouth across her cheeks. ''Come on, I want to see a smile as big as a Cheshire cat's before I go. You were getting too maudlin.''

''You ought to have been a shrink!'' She bared her teeth exaggeratedly for him.

His hands, which had dropped to her shoulders, now slowly slid upward, fingertips almost touching on her nape, thumbs lightly caressing the hollows of her throat, until he was barely cupping her face in his broad palms. There was a moment that was pure time warp, when nothing existed or mattered but the close-ness of two people discovering that they are strongly attracted to each other. It was more potent even than that morning.

Then Melinda, waking as though from a daydream to find Kyle's lips ominously close, drew in a sharp breath. She jerked her head away and took an alarmed step backward. Kyle's hands fell loosely to his sides.

Melinda, more rattled than she cared to admit, invented. "I've a few phone calls to make...."

He shoved his hands into his pockets as if to keep them out of mischief. "Yes, of course."

"Arrangements for the reunion," she explained.

"You mean the hens' party you told me about the other day."

"Yes. They'll be here at the weekend."

"I hope I'll be invited to meet them."

"Come for coffee on Sunday morning. I'm sure they'll be thrilled to see you again."

Idly she wondered what Katherine, Rose and Sylvana would make of him now. Katherine was divorced, too, and lived in Sydney.

Kyle moved around her to the door. "Congratulations again on the medal, Melly." He paused, then added, "You really ought to celebrate. What about going into Perth tonight for dinner?"

Melinda hadn't expected that. "Tonight?"

"Why not? It's not every day you win gold medals."

She was touched. "That's kind of you, Kyle."

"I'll pick you up about six-thirty."

The sound of the screen door slamming and foot-steps made them both turn. Matthew's anxious face was framed in the doorway. He looked taken aback to see his father.

"Ah, Matthew," Kyle said. "I forgot to remind you that you have an appointment with the dentist this afternoon."

Matthew caught Melinda's eye and grimaced. "I just remembered. Rocky was going to run me home."

"Well, there's no need for him to now," said Kyle, looking his son over critically. He commented, "I think you've just got time to shower and brush your teeth."

Melinda was struck as she had been before by the brusqueness in Kyle's voice when he spoke to his son, as though he was speaking to a stranger, not his own flesh and blood. Yet there was no doubt that the child was his, she thought, exchanging a sympathetic smile with the dark-haired little boy with Kyle's eyes and features that were already showing the strong lines of his father's. His hair, too, was Kyle's—thick and wavy, with a wayward lock on his forehead that he pushed back with the same impatient gesture as his father. And he had the same dusky olive complexion.

Melinda said, "It'll soon be over, Matthew. Be brave."

"Come on," Kyle urged. "Or you'll be late." He strode out, leaving his son to follow.

Matthew scampered towards the big, dark blue Commodore parked outside. Melinda waited for them to drive off.

"See you," Matthew called, waving madly out the car window.

"Don't bite the dentist!" shouted Melinda.

Kyle gave her a lazy salute.

Why hadn't she politely refused his invitation? Melinda thought in sudden panic as she returned indoors. She didn't want to go out to dinner with Kyle. Yes, you do, contradicted a loud voice in her head. She conducted this cerebral argument for most of the afternoon, vowing one minute to call him as soon as she thought he'd be back from the dentist's, then berating herself as an idiot. What in heaven's name was wrong with having dinner with Kyle?

She spent the afternoon on the accounts, but too often gazed out the window, down the long rows of vines with their bright green new growth seeming to sprout by the minute in the spring sunshine. She kept smiling to herself every time she reached for the letter and read again about the gold medal.

The letter, Kyle and Matthew's interruption and Kyle's unexpected invitation had banished from her mind temporarily the imminent fate of Jarrahwood, but during the afternoon it returned with devastating force. She let her gaze roam down over the vineyard to the belt of trees, unable to imagine a landscape without it.

She chewed her pen. Could she afford to buy the property herself? The vineyard's finances weren't in all that great shape. There was already a mortgage on Riversham, raised to buy new fermentation tanks and a modern crusher. But the new acres of Pinot Noir would be fruiting this year, as well as the Cabernet Sauvignon and the Malbec her father had had high hopes for. And with a gold medal under her belt, her wines would sell better. Maybe the bank would lend her the money on the strength of future vintages.

"I'll go and see them tomorrow," she decided, and when she left the office later in the day to get ready for her date with Kyle she was feeling more than a little optimistic, and was full of fresh plans. "We ought to take the Cornichons out," she muttered under the shower, thinking aloud. "They're old and not very productive anymore. We could replant with more Malbec or Sauvignon, even Shiraz." She experienced a pang over the Cornichon. They had been a popular table grape once, but were no longer. Because she could draw faces in the heavy bloom on the dark purple grapes, they had been one of her childhood favorites. But if her light red wine did take off as she hoped, she would need to make more new plantings of the varieties she needed for the blend.

"I'll talk it over with Gianni and Rocky," she said decisively, and then giving in to sentiment, retracted a little. "Maybe we could keep those few Cornichons on the trellis by the house...."

In her mind, the gold-medal wine was already reaping her a fortune and she had bought Jarrahwood and repaid the bank in no time flat. By the time she'd zipped up the blue silk dress she'd chosen to wear, tamed her hair into a soft frame for her face and carefully made up her eyes and mouth, Kyle was driving into the yard and tooting for her. She slipped the matching blue silk jacket over her shoulders and slid her feet into high-heeled sandals. She entered the kitchen just as Kyle came through the vestibule calling out for her.

She stopped in her tracks and stared at him. Gone were the faded jeans she had been accustomed to seeing him in. He was immaculately attired in a silver-gray suit with a dark maroon shirt and gray tie. Every nerve in her body tautened. She was reacting so strongly to him it appalled her. That this much physical attraction could have survived all these years was preposterous. Because that's all it was. She had no illusions that her past romance with Kyle had been any more than just a youthful passion—the first time, in fact, that she had fallen in love.

Chapter Two

He was staring, too, and with a strange fleeting perplexity in his eyes. "It's a long while since I saw you all dressed up," he said with a slow smile of approval.

Melinda screwed up her face. "Thanks. You were expecting jeans and T-shirt?" Her laughter didn't quite level out the tremor in her voice, and her fingers tightened on the strap of her purse. This was the first time she'd been out on a date with Kyle since he'd come back, and it felt peculiar. After so many years she seemed to have forgotten how to behave. Which was idiotic. She'd been out with other men. For a long moment she remained glued to the same spot on the floor, as though waiting for someone to wind her up.

Kyle came closer and looked down at her. He touched her arm. "Ready?" She nodded. "Then let's go."

Firm fingers through soft silk made Melinda's skin prickle with a warmth that spread like a blush. She lifted her feet from the floor and made them follow him out to the car. Kyle held the passenger door open. Getting into the car was like stepping through a revolving door and finding oneself back in the past, Melinda thought as she sank into the soft upholstery. Kyle deftly tucked a swirl of skirt in after her, briefly brushing her thigh as he did so. Melinda's senses reacted even to that small intimacy. She was allowing herself to become too physically aware of him. No more dates after tonight, she decided as he slid in beside her. Not that he would invite her out again. Tonight was just a special occasion because of her gold medal.

"I've heard that a new hotel that recently opened down by the river has an excellent restaurant," Kyle remarked as the big car negotiated the long driveway to the road.

"You haven't opened one yourself in Perth?" she queried.

"Not yet."

"I suppose you're always on the lookout to extend your empire."

He turned his head briefly with a reproachful look. "You make me sound like a corporate raider."

"I imagine it could be hard to resist opportunities," Melinda said.

He laughed dryly. "Does that mean you'll buy Heronvale if it comes up for sale?"

Melinda was shocked. "You're going to sell Heronvale?" Then she added, "Well, I suppose you

wouldn't want it, and nor would Mario and Elizabeth. What does your mother want to do?''

Her gaze was drawn to the strong lines of his profile. He'd been a bony, somewhat angular youth, but
now the frame was more fleshed out, emphasizing his
maturity.

He waited a moment or two before answering and
Melinda thought she'd been presumptuous and he was
snubbing her. Finally he said, ''She doesn't want to
sell. I'm doing my best to convince her that it's the best
course.''

''She's lived there a long time,'' Melinda sympa-
thized. ''It's only natural she wouldn't want to leave.''

A harsh little laugh preceded his answer. ''You valley people are as hard to shift as an old red gum
stump.''

''What do your brother and sister think about it?''
Like Kyle, they had left the valley.

''They've delegated me to sort everything out and
do what's best. They agree that Mama should move to
some place more convenient, but she won't hear of it.
She wants to continue to run the vineyard herself,
which is ridiculous.''

''Why?''

Kyle turned briefly with a twisted grin. ''My mother
may not be a feminist, but she has a mind of her own.
I daresay she thinks if you can run Riversham, she can
cope with Heronvale. But you had a lot more practical experience with your father before you took over.
Mama never took a very active part in the vineyard.
I'm not sure she realizes what she would be taking on.
Heronvale is rather run-down, I'm afraid. My father
was ill, I now know, long before anyone realized it. All

that indigestion he complained about was really angina pain. A lot of renovation and repairs need to be done. Much of our equipment needs replacing. Not to mention a fair acreage of vines. It would require considerable capital.''

Melinda made a daring suggestion. ''Couldn't you invest in it yourself? After all, you'll be one of the beneficiaries in the end, won't you?'' She was certain he could afford to set Heronvale on its feet without any trouble. She went on, ''And then your mother can stay there as long as she wants.''

He showed only wry amusement at her unsolicited advice. ''Trust you to be on her side!''

Melinda responded heatedly. ''Look, I know it would be very convenient for you and Elizabeth and Mario to move her out to a nice little suburban home in Heronbush or Perth, but that would be cruel. Her roots are here, Kyle. She's lived here for most of her life.''

''She has friends in Heronbush and Perth. She could see more of them, have a busy social life, if she'd move. She doesn't realize yet how lonely she's going to be.''

''She has Rosa. Anyway, she doesn't have to be lonely. She can hop in her car anytime and drive to Perth, just as she's always done.''

''And when she's too old to drive anymore?''

Melinda was beginning to feel angry with him. ''She can cross that bridge when she comes to it. If she doesn't want to sell up and move now, you shouldn't try to force her to, just because it would suit you. You're as bad as poor old Mrs. Marchant's grasping sons." She stopped abruptly, afraid that she had overstepped the mark.

Kyle, however, was not riled, merely curious. "Oh, and what have the Marchants got to do with it?"

"Nothing, except that they've coerced the old lady into putting Jarrahwood up for sale. It's going to be auctioned soon. And she's to go into a retirement village. It's true she's a good bit older than your mother, but it's the same thing. She doesn't want to go. Why should people be pushed around just to suit their children? Their roots are here and they should be allowed to stay where they're happiest."

"But it's probably the most sensible thing to do," he contended.

"Being sensible isn't always being happy," said Melinda stubbornly. "Just because you couldn't wait to leave the valley, just because a lot of other people like Sam and Morris Marchant were the same, doesn't mean the rest of us ought to follow suit. Surely you don't need to make us conform in order to justify your own decisions."

"That's a bizarre notion."

They were almost quarreling, Melinda realized, but she was unable to hold back. "Is it? People often feel less guilty about what they do if everyone else is doing it, too." She glanced at him and wondered if the jerky muscular movement in his jaw was significant. Had she touched a raw nerve? The atmosphere in the car was now overheating. It was hardly the way to start an evening that was meant to be a celebration. She shouldn't have let him provoke her.

Kyle suddenly laughed softly. "It cuts both ways, Melly." He swept a brief look in her direction.

"Maybe those who stay put would feel better about it if everyone else did."

"Touché," she conceded.

Melinda's eyes were fixed on his hands, lying lightly on the wheel but in full control. He'd always been a good driver, she reflected, exhibiting a kind of grace in his smooth handling of a car. Reckless sometimes, though, she recalled, her heart missing a beat at the memory of speeding with Kyle along valley roads.

"Have you been to the Western Star?" Kyle asked.

"No, I haven't," Melinda said. "I expect it's rather expensive."

"Only the best for a gold medalist!" He turned slightly and his smile teased. "This is a celebration, remember? With you all dressed up like that, I must take you somewhere glamorous."

"You've become very gallant," Melinda remarked dryly, which made him chuckle. She added, "I don't mind where we go. It's nice to be going out at all."

"Don't you have any social life? You know the saying about all work and no play."

She realized he must think her dull. "There isn't so much social activity in the valley these days," she admitted reluctantly. "Most people prefer to go to Heronbush or Perth for entertainment. There's even a disco in Heronbush now, so we don't have weekly dances in the old church hall anymore."

"You must have boyfriends who take you to town sometimes?"

"Now and then," she agreed.

"Anyone special?" he asked.

"Not at the moment." Rustling the material of her outfit, she added flippantly, "I go to lots of weddings, of course. I bought this for one. It cost an arm and a leg but it comes in handy for other special occasions."

He said smoothly, "I'm glad I qualify as a special occasion."

She couldn't let him get away with that. "Everything else was in the wash. I stretched a point."

He grinned at her teasing put-down. "Whose wedding did you buy it for?"

"Maria Torino and Alex Manetti. You won't remember them. They were still in primary school when you left."

"I know the families. I haven't been away so long I've forgotten everything about Heron Valley," he chided.

"I thought your life must be so full of other more important things." Her words were not coming out the way she intended. She wasn't relaxed and she sounded cynical.

Kyle swept over the remark. "I suppose it was a full-scale Italian wedding?"

"Absolutely. Everyone had a wonderful time. Tradition isn't quite dead in the valley yet. The only difference is that nobody uses the old hall anymore for weddings. They go to Heronbush to the smart new reception center. I'll be going to another one soon. Rocky's young sister, Tanya. She's marrying a solicitor."

"From Heronbush?"

"No, Perth."

The car swung wide around a bend in the road, headlights beaming through a cluster of gum trees on the shoulder, and Melinda was jerked toward Kyle, her shoulder momentarily bumping his before the seat belt bounced her back. She found her instinctively flung hand on his thigh and quickly withdrew it, hoping he wouldn't think the intimacy had been deliberate.

"So another one leaves the valley. What about Maria and Alex? Does Alex work in the vineyards?"

"No. He's a trainee manager with a wine merchant in Perth."

"Young people need to spread their wings," Kyle said.

"Not all," she defended. "Some stay, some go. Alex's older brother will take over from their father."

Kyle glanced at her. "If you'd had any older or younger brothers to take over Riversham, would you have left?"

Gone with him when he'd wanted her to? Was that what he meant? She said levelly, "My roots have always been in the valley."

They were nearing Perth now, passing from rural darkness into brightly lit suburbs, and the traffic was heavier. Kyle lapsed into silence.

"The city's changed a great deal in the past decade." His sudden remark startled her as they crossed the causeway over the Swan River and approached the city.

"Yes. Every year more skyscrapers." She supposed it couldn't be all new to him. She knew he'd been back a few times on business and to see his parents, but when he'd visited Heronvale he had never looked her up. The first time they'd spoken in ten years had been at his father's funeral. To her amazement, because she'd been very nervous of the unavoidable encounter, they hadn't even been awkward with each other. Time had wiped out the bitterness. Or so it had seemed.

He peered ahead at a road sign. "I think we turn off here."

In a few moments they were leaving the car in the hotel's basement parking ramp and going up in the elevator to the Pink Cockatoo. The restaurant drew a silent gasp from Melinda. In mimicry of the cockatoo's plumage, it was decorated entirely in pink and white with small touches of yellow. The walls were papered with a design of abstract feathers, and one prominent panel displayed an enormous, amazingly lifelike pink-and-white cockatoo.

The bar was separated from the dining area by screens painted with stylized birds. Kyle made straight for a table near a window that commanded a breathtaking view across the city, with the river below shimmering with reflections of the city lights. To Melinda the scene brought a sudden sharp yearning, a memory of long-ago dates with Kyle before their romance had ended.

A waiter asking what they would like to drink brought her back to earth and then Kyle's eye caught hers before she could look away again, causing another stone in her wall of defense to collapse. The old chemistry was still potent, but she wasn't going to start falling for Kyle again. They were chalk and cheese, as she'd told Rocky. She was a valley girl and he was a man of the world. He'd be back in his world in a few weeks and this time he wouldn't even be wanting her to go with him. She wondered if there was anyone special yet waiting to take the place of Gina Rainham.

Kyle said, "I nearly forgot. Matthew sent his love and congratulations. He said to buy you a chocolate ice cream because it's your favorite and he'll pay me out of his pocket money."

Melinda smiled affectionately. "Isn't that nice! We might have to go to a milk bar later for it, though, if they don't have it here."

"And you wouldn't pretend, would you?" He angled a questioning look at her.

"You should never deceive children, because they learn not to trust you if you do," Melinda said.

Kyle nodded. "They seem to have a sixth sense about pretensions."

"I guess Matthew's had a pretty rough time," Melinda ventured. "All that fighting for custody couldn't have been fun."

Kyle looked momentarily angry. "It wasn't. It was hell. You can hardly blame him for resenting me."

"He's lost his sense of security, Kyle. He needs a lot of loving to restore his faith in you."

"I have so little time." Kyle raked his hair distractedly. "I'm afraid I'm not a very good father, Mel. But heaven knows, his mother would be worse."

"Maybe you just need to sort your priorities out a bit. Or maybe you should be thinking of marrying again. Matthew could do with a permanent person in his life," Melinda suggested, then bit her lip. He was bound to resent advice, especially such a personal kind, even if his words had invited it.

"I can't marry just anyone to provide Matthew with a stepmother."

"Of course not, but you could be considering it, instead of just looking at women who please *you*."

And that, she thought, wondering what had got into her to cause such forthright speaking, was downright offensive. She waited for his wrath but Kyle seemed not to be offended.

"There haven't been any women for quite some time," he said, meeting her eyes with an emphatic look. "I wanted to give all my spare time to Matthew, but it isn't easy. I suppose he blames me for the marriage breakup, even though she walked out on me."

"He's probably just confused and very lonely," Melinda suggested, basing her opinion on what she had experienced so far of the boy. "He wants to escape from the hurt, but he can't. He's bound to be torn, Kyle, between you and Gina. He's suffering a loyalty crisis. His way out of the dilemma is to ignore the source of the hurt and find solace elsewhere."

The anger Melinda expected still did not come. Kyle looked thoughtful, then said, "Rosa told me about your taking him for a picnic. He didn't tell me himself. He rarely tells me anything. He had a great time, apparently."

"We both did." Melinda smiled at the recollection. "It was very impromptu. We packed some sandwiches and drinks in a cooler and went down to Jarrahwood. I scared the daylights out of him with tales of the old bushranger's hut and ghosts. I was half expecting you to tell me off for giving him nightmares, but he loved it. We did some bird-watching and then swung on the old tire over the river and I fell in...."

Kyle's face was bursting with amusement. "How old are you, Melly?"

She blushed. "Oh, twenty-nine going on ten, I guess."

Kyle laughed and lifted his glass. "Here's to you, Melinda Richardson. May there be many more gold medals. I'm sure Riversham and you have a great future. But you really ought to get married and raise a football team. You clearly have quite a way with small boys."

Melinda murmured, "Thanks, Kyle," and took a sip of the pale gold sherry. Its warmth seemed to course though all her veins and her tension quickly eased.

Kyle directed the conversation away from his personal dilemmas. "I noticed you've made some fairly recent plantings down on the flats."

"You've been walking by the river?"

"Jogging. Early in the morning." He grinned. "Reminiscing in old haunts. I haven't been game to swing on the old tire, though."

Melinda sighed. "It's not quite the same when you're grown up." A rush of memory made her color faintly. The riverbank had also been a favorite lovers' lane for local youth. Kissing in the long grass with Kyle was suddenly a vivid image in her mind. She wondered if similar images were in his. Or had he forgotten? A lot of water had flowed under the bridge since they'd kissed on the riverbank. And their romance hadn't been important, not really—especially not to him, as she'd later discovered. It had just been a youthful passion.

Kyle asked, "What are you growing down there? More Shiraz?"

Melinda welcomed the invitation to talk shop. "Some. We grubbed out the old muscats which were no longer cropping well and put in some Shiraz and some Malbec, but it's mainly Pinot Noir. It was Dad's idea. . . ." Her voice wavered before she went on. "If only he could have lived long enough to see the light red he believed in so much win a medal." Her eyes misted over and she took a gulp of sherry.

"I'm sure he'd be proud of the way you're carrying on the vineyard," Kyle said.

"I've got quite a few plans for it," Melinda told him and rushed into enthusiastic explanations, then stopped herself. "Sorry. You can't be interested in all that."

"On the contrary, I'm very interested. It sounds as though you have the next decade well and truly planned," he said, adding, "but let's go and eat and you can tell me more about it over dinner."

During the meal they continued discussing vines and wine making. Melinda was surprised to find that Kyle had retained a real interest in the business despite having abandoned it, so with this encouragement she had no compunction in talking about her favorite subject.

"You talk almost as though you miss the vineyards," she dared to tease him once.

He laughed but didn't deny it. "I'm still fascinated by the processes. Wine making takes a great deal of dedication."

"It can become a bit of an obsession," Melinda admitted.

"That's true of any occupation, I'm afraid." He tipped a little more of the crisp dry white wine they were drinking into Melinda's glass. "You know, Bram would be tickled pink about your gold medal success, Melly. There can't be many women wine makers in Australia, especially ones with gold medals to their credit."

Melinda was flattered by his compliments, but modesty made her insist, "I can't claim all the credit, Kyle. Dad started it off, and without Gianni I couldn't have carried on. I'm still learning."

"And from what Gianni tells me, learning very fast. I don't think he lied when he told me that the light red was entirely yours. He said you tended those grapes to the peak of perfection and were meticulous at every stage of the fermentation and blending. I'm sure that you well deserve the accolade."

Melinda conceded, "Well, I—I did take over from Dad when he got sick, and I babied that vintage like the grapes had been born premature! Actually, I was lucky. I was able to pick at exactly the right time—you know, when the sugar's at precisely the right level. I was out there checking the crop on almost a daily basis, and I got a crick in my neck watching the sky for weather." She paused and added anxiously, "Kyle, I want to continue to make that wine to a consistent quality. I do so much want to make it a success—for Dad."

"Continue to devote yourself to it," Kyle answered slowly. "And you're bound to succeed."

Melinda went on eagerly, "I must get down to work on the new labels. And I mustn't forget the other wines in pampering my new baby. Our Riesling is improving all the time." Her face lit up. "Maybe I'll win a medal for that next."

"Careful, you'll become a workaholic."

She pulled a face. "I already am. But I'd hazard a guess you're worse than I am. Tell me more about the hotel business. It must be very competitive."

He shrugged. "Long hours, plenty of headaches, that about sums it up."

"Haven't you recently bought a new place on the Gold Coast?" Melinda asked, remembering reading about it in the business pages of the daily newspaper.

He nodded and told her a little about the venture, but he seemed reluctant to talk about himself and kept switching the conversation back to her.

When the waiter brought the menus back for them to choose dessert, Melinda was delighted to find a chocolate ice cream confection.

"Not quite what Matthew probably had in mind." She laughed. "But it sounds gorgeous, if highly fattening and intoxicating."

"I don't think you need to worry about the former," Kyle said.

When Melinda had finished the luscious sweet, she sighed with satisfaction. "You can tell Matthew that it was the best chocolate ice cream I've ever eaten," she said. "And the most expensive. I hope he can afford it! Thank him very much for it, won't you, Kyle?"

Kyle smiled, oddly touched by her simple pleasure and her genuine desire to please Matthew. He ordered coffee, then asked, "Would you like to go dancing?"

Melinda glanced at her watch. "It's getting late...."

"We won't dance till dawn," he promised with a teasing smile.

She gave in. "All right. This *is* a celebration. Where shall we go?"

"There's a nightclub right here in the hotel."

So he'd already checked it out. They left the restaurant and took an elevator down to the nightclub, which was already crowded. As they entered, a singer, looking and sounding like Madonna, her sequined dress shimmering in the spotlight, had everyone's attention.

As they were ushered to a table, the singer finished her last number, bowed and left the stage to the sound of enthusiastic applause. The spotlight went out and couples moved onto the dance floor.

Kyle offered his hand and Melinda rose, taking it lightly, letting him guide her between the tables to the dance floor. "Do you still tread on toes?" she asked flippantly.

"I might have crippled valley girls at barn dances in my teens," he admitted, "but I'm more proficient now." He drew her into his arms. "I still prefer the old-fashioned way, don't you?"

Melinda wasn't sure that she did. Dancing with space between them would have been less alarming to her senses. At first she couldn't relax. She was all too aware of his warm fingers entwined with hers, the firmness of his broad palm spread comfortably across the small of her back and the tangy perfume of his after-shave.

"Your hand's cold," he said suddenly, chafing her fingers.

"I hadn't noticed." It must be the tension, she thought.

"Cold hands, warm heart, they say." Were the dark eyes teasing or serious?

He pulled her closer, and a small shiver of something more alarming than cold ran through her. If racing made a heart warm, then he was right, Melinda thought. Hers was pumping as if she'd just run up several flights of stairs. And as Kyle's hand slid farther around her waist, drawing her closer until her breasts and thighs were brushing against him, she searched for something to say, but couldn't even think of a flippant remark. They swayed gently amid the crowd of other dancers to the rhythm of a blues number, played so plaintively by horns and saxophones that Melinda almost wanted to weep. Instinctively she nestled against Kyle for comfort, and was rewarded with a tightening of his arms around her. If she closed her eyes, it was just like old times....

It must have been the wine, Melinda thought, as a moment or two later she realized with a shock that she was resting her cheek against his chest and that the rhythmic thumping in her ear was nothing to do with the jazz percussionist. It was Kyle's heartbeat, strong, regular and dangerously hypnotic. When the music stopped at last she didn't know whether to be relieved or disappointed.

As they reached their table, a waiter bearing a tray of glasses offered, "Champagne, sir?"

Melinda watched the bubbles in her champagne and wondered if she ought to drink any more. She was beginning to feel a bit too bubbly herself.

After the next cabaret act, she was feeling so sleepy she could scarcely keep from yawning, so she suggested they go home. "It's a long way and it's very late," she murmured apologetically.

Kyle did not seem to mind. "Ready when you are."

In the car Melinda promptly fell asleep and didn't wake until Kyle lifted her out back at Riversham. To him, she was as light and fragile as a child and involuntarily he brushed his lips across her tumbled mass of satiny hair.

"Hey! Put me down!" The cool night air revived Melinda. She realized where they were and heaved a sigh of relief. Momentarily, the stars were spinning in the heavens and her head sagged against Kyle's chest, where the vibrations of his laughter sounded pleasantly in her ear.

"I'm going to put you to bed." He strode toward the house.

"The hell you are! I don't need you to—" She tried to wriggle out of his grasp. "Where's my purse? My key?"

He set her down. "Right here." He handed over both purse and key, and kept one hand on her arm to steady her. "Sorry I rummaged in your handbag, but you were dead to the world and I hadn't the heart to disturb you. Now, since you're awake you can let yourself in."

The stars stopped spinning for Melinda. "Thanks. Sorry if I wasn't much company on the way home." She felt that her going to sleep might seem like ingratitude, so she said, "Would you like some coffee?"

"It's three in the morning."

She grinned. "I think I need some myself."

He hesitated for a moment while she opened the door, then followed her inside. Was he reading her

rightly or wrongly? he thought. Was she just in an ex-
pansive mood because of the champagne, or was there
more to it than that? She wasn't quite the same person he'd known years ago. His eyes and certain of his
other senses told him that.

"Go into the living room, Kyle," Melinda said,
"and put your feet up. Take your shoes off if you like.
I'm going to." She kicked hers into a corner and padded on stocking feet into the kitchen. "I won't be
long."

She felt fine now, quite sober. She also felt happy
and generous and affectionate toward Kyle. She was
truly grateful for the night out to celebrate her gold
medal. She made the coffee and when she carried it in
she almost joined him on the couch, but an instinc-
tive wariness made her sit in a chair on the other side
of the coffee table.

"It was a great night out," she said. "Thanks for
helping me celebrate in style."

His eyes were shadowed and Melinda wasn't sure of
their message. However, it was gradually sinking in
that inviting him in for coffee at three in the morning
might not have been a wise impulse, that he might be
expecting more than she had intended. Maybe he always expected some reward for taking a woman out.

"My pleasure, ma'am," he mocked gently.

Melinda stretched out and contemplated her toes.
She felt more lighthearted than light-headed. They
talked idly, and soon Melinda began to yawn again. At
that point Kyle rose, saying, "You'd better get to bed.
Thanks for the coffee. I'll be going."

Melinda stood up to see him out. There was no invitation in her eyes, but Kyle suddenly couldn't help

himself. He reached for her like a drowning man, holding her head against him, running urgent fingers along her spine, spreading a palm over her breast, soft and enticing under its silken covering. As he tilted her chin and claimed her mouth, he felt her resistance crumble. She molded her body willingly to his, and like her he was breathless at the speeding desire that was hurling them into the realms of rapture.

Melinda felt the storm rising inside her, a whirlwind of conflicting emotions. When their lips parted to draw breath, she managed to rescue her willpower. "Kyle, this is crazy. . . ."

"I know." His voice was low, husky and subtly persuasive.

"The champagne has gone to our heads."

He stroked her hair, traced the shape of her ears with light fingertips and gently massaged the sensitive hollows above her collarbone. She was getting to him in ways she never had even when they'd been in love all those years ago.

"You know I want to make love to you, don't you?" Kyle whispered, and subtle body language confirmed it.

Melinda shook her head. "No, Kyle."

"Why not? It'd be so good. We both know that."

"But too fleeting," she managed to say. "Too temporary, Kyle. Brief affairs are not for me."

"It could be permanent—if you'd come back with me."

Melinda fell the rest of the way back to earth. "Kyle, you don't mean that. That's not what you want."

She was right. He hadn't meant to say it, but the words had come in spite of himself. "Melly..." He couldn't explain. He'd never felt so unclear about what he did want.

For a brief, electrifying moment Melinda saw herself running away with Kyle, leaving everything behind, all her obligations, all her doubts and fears, chancing everything to be with him—but that was fantasy. Kyle didn't love her. She didn't love him. Passion wasn't enough. With an effort of will, she twisted away from him. "It's easy, Kyle, at moments like this, to say and do things both of us would regret. Let's not get too carried away."

His answer was to draw her back to him, holding her so tightly against him she could sense the urgency of his desire, and despite herself her own need escalated to match his. As his mouth moved persuasively on hers, she felt her willpower ebbing away.

But not quite. Melinda scrambled desperately for the last shreds of resistance, until a cold wave of sanity cleared her brain completely. She twisted away from him again. "I'm sorry, Kyle. If I misled you, I'm sorry."

"Are you always such a tease?" The harsh words were to disguise his frustration and the emotional turmoil he hadn't expected. Ten years ago he'd been in love with her. Or thought he was. But if he had been, would he have left her? And if she'd loved him, wouldn't she have gone with him? At the time his desire to leave the valley, hers to remain, had caused a conflict to which there had been no solution but parting. And nothing had really changed. She was as wedded to the valley as ever. Everything she'd said tonight had confirmed it. He'd aroused her passionate instincts, she'd fired him, but that was all. The die had been cast for them long ago. Why was he even thinking about it? And saying such a stupid thing to her....

Melinda clenched her hands together and unwittingly put his own thoughts into words. "Kyle, it's not surprising, I suppose, that we still strike sparks off each other. I shouldn't have invited you in."

For a long moment the air between them was as supercharged as though a thunderstorm was imminent, then Kyle dragged his gaze from Melinda's face.

"I guess I'd better be going." He strode to the door, hesitated and turned around as though he had something more to say. All he said in the end was a brusque, "Thanks for the coffee."

Melinda did not see him out. She held her breath until she heard the back door slam behind him. Then, as the tension eased, she burst into tears. The sound of Kyle's car driving away was a painful echo of his going ten years ago.

Chapter Three

Awake at dawn, Melinda rose early as usual, but she moved mechanically to shower and dress and have breakfast. She could not help brooding over the stormy conclusion to last night's date with Kyle. Even so, fragments of the evening kept taunting her with remembered pleasure and brought an involuntary smile to her lips. She deeply regretted that it had ended so acrimoniously, but that was her own fault for unwittingly giving Kyle the wrong impression. She could hardly blame him if he kept out of her way for the rest of the time he was at Heronvale.

"Which will be just as well," she told herself and deliberately switched her mind to the problem of Jarrahwood.

Her attachment to Jarrahwood was largely an emotional one, she knew, but the area also had intrinsic environmental value. It was the last virgin bush left in the valley and it was a sanctuary for a wide variety of wildlife. It would be criminal, Melinda firmly believed, to destroy such a unique environment. But it was private property and the owners of private property were permitted, rightly, to do as they wished with their freehold land.

After swallowing a hasty breakfast she called Polly and as usual walked the dog down through the vines toward Jarrahwood. The air was dewy, and the budding leaves and curling tendrils on the vines were spangled with droplets. Spiders had been busy weaving overnight and their webs sparkled in the first rays of the sun, between the gnarled branches of the old vines she intended to remove soon. It was her world and she had never yearned, as her friends had, for any other... which was what made her recent restlessness inexplicable.

Polly suddenly barked at something unseen and scattered a screeching flock of "greenies," brilliant emerald-green ring-necked parrots, which flew low overhead into the sun. Kookaburras reaffirmed their territorial rights with shouts of raucous laughter, and other bird songs mingled melodiously as Melinda walked briskly into the trees, inhaling the pungent early-morning perfume of damp leaves and earth, faintly eucalypt.

Her artist's eye was keenly aware of the wildflowers that were daily opening up in the spring weather. All around her was the flamboyant yellow of bush buttercups, the pink and blue hues of Star of Bethlehem, the brilliant indigo pea flowers of the Hovea and the vivid red-and-green kangaroo paws that crowded open spaces with their velvety blooms. But it was the

ground orchids she searched for diligently, the cowslips, the ones called spider, donkey, potato and other
quaint names. They were shy flowers, easily missed by
the unobservant. She trod carefully so as not to tram-
ple any, and occasionally bent to look more closely at
a catspaw or a glossy purple enamel orchid. It was
difficult to select which ones to feature on her wine
labels, for which she would reproduce their delicate
tones in watercolors.

The flower labels would be an attractive indication
of the region where the wine came from. Jarrahwood
bush, untouched for generations, was a treasure house
of the many species of wildflowers for which the state
of Western Australia was famous, and from which it
derived its title of "wildflower state." It was also a
habitat for many birds and some animals. Even if no
one else ever appreciated its beauties, she thought,
surely it had a right to exist for its own sake and that
of its natural inhabitants. The earth needed some small
corners that were safe from human exploitation.

As she stood quietly absorbing the beauty of her
surroundings, a sudden movement drew her gaze and
she caught a glimpse of three gray kangaroos bounding gracefully through the trees. It had been a while
since she had seen any kangaroos in Jarrahwood. They
were one more tangible reason for its preservation.
Melinda flung her arms around a young tree. "I won't
let it happen," she promised fiercely.

Back at the homestead she called her bank and
made an appointment to see the manager the following morning. Organizing finance was the first hurdle
to overcome, and then she would have to try to per-

suade Mrs. Marchant, which meant her sons, too, to sell before auction.

Matthew did not come over to Riversham that day and Melinda felt a twinge of conscience. Was Kyle keeping him away on purpose?

The next morning when Melinda went to get the car out of the garage to drive to Heronbush, she found it wouldn't start. Rocky was working on one of the farthest parts of the property, so she couldn't ask him to look at it for her. Gianni knew all about wine, and wine-making equipment, but not much about cars. To Melinda, all engines were a complete mystery.

"Never mind, I'll take the pickup," she decided, making her way back to the garage. At once she realized that she couldn't do that because it was still parked in the yard, jacked up for some repair Rocky hadn't finished yet.

"Damn!" she exploded in irritation. She couldn't borrow Rocky's truck because only half an hour ago Gerry, one of her two other permanent workers, had taken it to pick up some fertilizer. For once there wasn't a drivable vehicle on the property. She tried the car again, but to no avail.

"Wretched thing!" Now she'd have to call Mr. Cotham and cancel her appointment.

Then Melinda's eyes rested on her bicycle, which she hadn't used much recently. She glanced at her watch. She could still be on time if she cycled to Heronbush. It would take her about an hour, which would mean doing her shopping after going to the bank rather than before as she'd planned. She wheeled the bicycle out and pumped up the tires. Then she ran down to tell Gianni where she was going.

Melinda loved the winding road to Heronbush. It was very scenic, especially now with the vines coming into leaf and the red loam between the rows newly turned. She loved seeing, from the crests of hills, the whole valley spread out before her, with glimpses of the river winding through it. The surrounding hills seemed to hem in the long rows of vines as though to stop them escaping. She had cycled a lot in her younger days, sometimes with Kyle. . . .

As though a mere memory could conjure him up, Kyle's car suddenly drew up alongside Melinda with a tentative toot. She dismounted as he leaned across to wind down the window to speak to her.

"What's this? Training for the Tour de France?" There was no sign of lingering annoyance in his face, which she found a great relief.

"My car's out of order."

"Where are you off to?"

"Heronbush."

"Want to sling the boneshaker on the roof rack and climb aboard?"

"Thanks, but I'll make it on pedal power." Melinda was reluctant to ride in the car with him. She didn't want ever to be that close to him again.

Kyle was not slighted. "Well, if you're determined . . . I wouldn't want to deprive you of exercise."

He was friendly, but to Melinda's hypersensitive mind he sounded remote.

"Is Matthew all right?" she asked. "We didn't see him yesterday."

"He's fine, but I don't want him to wear out his welcome," Kyle said.

"Kyle, I've told you, Matthew is no trouble. He likes being with Rocky and he's great mates with Robert. Matthew is always welcome at Riversham." She emphasized "no trouble" and "always."

"That's good of you, Melly," he said, and then added quietly, "sorry about the other night. I guess I overreacted."

"We both did." Melinda managed to sound matter-of-fact, but for some unknown reason her eyes were misting over. "I'd better get going," she said quickly. "I've got an appointment with my bank manager."

"Sure I can't give you a lift?" he repeated. "I'm going to Heronbush."

"No. I'm nearly there. Thanks for the offer, though."

He didn't press her. "You're welcome. See you."

Had he added, "Take care,"? she wondered as the big car drove smoothly on and disappeared around a bend, or had she imagined it? She shrugged. So what if he had or he hadn't? Her warm glow was due to exertion, nothing else.

She put on a spurt and a few minutes later was securing her bike to a rack in the shopping mall. The bank was only a block away, and as she was now a few minutes late, Melinda rushed straight there. She was relieved to find that Mr. Cotham still had another customer with him. That gave her time to get her breath back and marshal her facts and arguments in favor of the bank granting her a loan.

When she finally walked into his office, Melinda was feeling highly optimistic. If she were on the other side of the manager's desk with the power to grant loans, she thought, she couldn't refuse. When Mr. Cotham heard her glowing account of Riversham's future prospects now that she'd won a gold medal for her wine, he would be bound to see her as a gilt-edged, no-risk investment. Head high, and feeling confident, she shook hands with him and sat in the chair he indicated.

"Well, Melinda, what can I do for you?" He'd known her since she was a little girl and since her father had died had taken a fatherly interest in her financial affairs. He was a friend as well as a bank manager, and Melinda was sure he would agree to her plan.

"I want to buy Jarrahwood," she said, coming straight to the point. "You know it's up for sale?"

His eyebrows shifted up a notch as he looked gravely at her. "You already have a mortgage, Melly," he reminded her cautiously.

"Yes, I know, but..." Enthusiastically she expounded on her future prospects in the wine market, produced the letter informing her about the gold medal, told him about the new vines that would be ready for picking this year and the replanting she intended to do. "I won't have any trouble repaying the loan," she said, displaying more confidence than she knew she had a right to feel.

He congratulated her on the gold medal, acknowledging the importance of medals in the Australian wine market, then said, "Jarrahwood is prime land.

It'll fetch a good price at auction—if it isn't snapped up beforehand."

"That's what I want to do." Melinda was beginning to feel impatient with his slow, cautious approach. "I want to get in first, before someone else does."

Mr. Cotham stroked his chin and said thoughtfully, "Well, as it adjoins your land it's certainly a practical proposition from that point of view, but I'm not sure I can agree with your optimism about increased output enabling you to service the loan. Interest rates are still high at the moment, Melly."

"I know. I thought if I could get an interest-only loan for a couple of years, and once my gold-medal wine takes off..."

He smiled indulgently at her enthusiasm, but was adamant. "You'd need capital to clear and plant, Melinda. Have you taken that into your calculations? Even I know that vines don't produce much return in the first few years."

Shocked by his assumption that she wanted the property for commercial reasons, Melinda hurriedly explained. "I've no intention of clearing it to plant vines, Mr. Cotham. I intend to keep Jarrahwood as it is."

He looked at her as though she was deranged. "Why? It's mainly bush, apart from the small patch of vines and the orchard. What use would it be to you?"

"Does everything have to have a commercial use? Jarrahwood is the only tract of untouched bush left in the valley, Mr. Cotham, and it should be preserved. It's environmentally important."

His bushy gray eyebrows rose. "You have an expert opinion on that?"

Melinda began to realize that her optimism had not been justified. "No, but—"

"It's possible you are exaggerating its importance," Mr. Cotham suggested, "out of mere sentimental attachment." He was becoming irritatingly patronizing. "I'm afraid you do not quite grasp the finer points of business, Melinda. I am only trying to advise you in your best interests."

Melinda felt her case crumbling before her eyes. She gave Mr. Cotham detailed arguments in favor of Jarrahwood's preservation, but she could see that he was not moved. He nodded patiently as she spoke, but it was obvious he considered her naive and impractical.

When she had finished, he said bluntly, "Melly, if I agreed to the bank lending you whatever sum you might need to buy Jarrahwood, that would be irresponsible of me because I am not convinced that you would be able to repay it. I would be failing my old friend Bram Richardson if I let you get into financial difficulties. Now, if you were planning to develop the land, then that might be another matter."

Melinda looked at him, bleakly. "In other words, no."

He nodded. "It's not a proposition I should feel happy about encouraging. It would be an enormous burden to you."

Melinda choked and bit her lip hard. She took a moment to control her emotions, then said, "If I go bankrupt, Mr. Cotham, that'll be my fault. You don't have to feel any obligation to my father. I'm an adult now and in charge of my own affairs. If I want to take risks—"

He became tight-lipped. "But I also have to consider the risk to the bank, my dear. I'm sorry, but the finance you would require would be considerable. You already have quite a large mortgage on Riversham, and you will be needing more capital to develop your gold-medal wine and market it. None of that will be possible if you tie yourself up with an unproductive property that will drain every cent of your profit. You'd be hanging a millstone around your neck, Melly."

He spoke kindly but firmly, and he probably had no alternative but to refuse her request. Melinda saw it was pointless to argue. She rose. "Thank you for your time, Mr. Cotham," she said formally. He was no longer an old friend of her father's. He was just an unfeeling manager of a bank that calculated the value of everything in dollars and cents.

He shook hands with her and tried to detain her with friendly conversation about other things. Melinda was relieved when his telephone rang. She muttered a brief goodbye and fled. Out in the street she began to fume, then despair.

"There must be a way," she muttered as she walked slowly along the main street. Just as she caught a glimpse of herself in a reflective shop window, scowling ferociously, a voice made her jump.

"So you made it!"

Melinda had almost walked into him. Kyle's arms closed briefly around her as he steadied her, then he let her go abruptly.

"Woolgathering," he cautioned, a humorous glint belying his stern tone, "is dangerous. You might have done me a serious injury."

She could only muster a weak smile. "I was inside the speed limit."

"But weaving all over the sidewalk."

"I wasn't!"

Their eyes met warmly for a moment, then Kyle's were shuttered again. "Have you had lunch yet?" he asked.

"I was just about to."

"So was I. Come on, let's get a counter lunch at the pub."

Melinda found herself whisked off to the hotel across the road before she could protest.

"You were looking fit to kill when you bumped into me," Kyle remarked as they perched on stools at the bar and ordered. "Problems?" He was surprised at how deeply moved he had been to see her looking unhappy. His resolve not to seek her company alone anymore had been nowhere to be seen when he'd heard himself inviting her to lunch with him. Careful, warned his inner mentor, don't get too involved.

"A big one," she confessed, more out of need to talk about it than any expectation of sympathy for her cause. "I want to buy Jarrahwood and my bank manager says no. Well, what he really says is that I wouldn't be able to service a loan so he won't give me a mortgage."

Kyle jumped to the obvious conclusion. "That gold medal really has gone to your head! Still, geographically it is logical to buy an adjoining property if you intend to expand." He laughed a little mockingly.

"Jarrahwood and Heronvale added on to Riversham would make you possibly the biggest in the valley." Seriously, he went on, "Well, why not? Nothing wrong with being ambitious. Your bank manager sounds a bit stuffy and small-town cautious. Why don't you go elsewhere?"

"Because I doubt if anyone else would be different." Melinda took a deep breath and told him the real reason she wanted to buy Jarrahwood. Then she waited for his derision.

He studied her face intently as she spoke, astonished to find that his assumption had been wrong. He said, "Melly, you're crazy."

"Yes, I know." She lifted her chin defiantly. "Don't lecture me, Kyle. Mr. Cotham's already done that. I'm a silly, sentimental fool." She buttered a roll savagely. "No, I am *not* a silly sentimental fool. There are enough vines in this valley. I don't want some tax-dodging hobby farmer desecrating the only bush left in the valley. That bush, Kyle, is a unique habitat for all kinds of wildlife. It's beautiful, it's environmentally important, it may even be ecologically unique." She thumped the handle of her knife on the counter for emphasis.

"You're raising your voice," Kyle murmured.

Melinda colored deeply. "Sorry." She placed the knife carefully across her plate and bit into her roll. It tasted like cardboard and she chewed slowly. Finally she swallowed and said, "Jarrahwood is part of the natural beauty of the valley. I don't want to see it destroyed. Once something like that is gone, you can't get it back."

Kyle was at a bit of a loss. She had floored him with her failure to fit his preconceived notion. Yet he should have realized how she would feel. "But what about Riversham?" he said. "You'll need to expand eventually and Jarrahwood would cost you less than Heronvale." He'd only been joking when he'd suggested she buy both, knowing she'd probably never be able to raise the capital.

Melinda bit her lip. "I don't want to get too big, Kyle. I'm not that ambitious. I wouldn't want to buy Heronvale even if I could. I want to stay small." She sighed. "You don't understand, do you? Jarrahwood is more important as a remnant of bushland than as a commercial proposition."

The despairing way her soft gray eyes accused him of soullessness wounded Kyle deeply. He wasn't without sensibilities just because he ran hotels for tourists. "Have you asked the opinion of expert environmentalists?"

"That's what Mr. Cotham asked me. No, not yet, but I will."

He smiled. "Maybe you'll end up waving placards and lying down in front of bulldozers." She probably would, too, he thought, with a sudden rush of affectionate concern. He could just see her—a five-foot-three, red-haired ball of fire brandishing a placard and shouting at bulldozer operators and crass developers, heedless of her own safety in pursuit of her principles.

"You really do think I'm ridiculous, don't you?" A flash of anger momentarily hid the despair clouding her eyes.

"I think you'll find that most people would regard the preservation of that tract of bush in a valley where good land is scarce as rather ridiculous." Kyle's hand rested briefly over hers. "Melly, I know it means a lot to you, but . . . you must be realistic."

She slumped, defeated. "I suppose I am a fool, Kyle."

He hated to see her defeated, but he didn't hold out much hope for her plan. He squeezed her hand. "You're not, Melly. You're just—well, different."

He wished he hadn't run into her. Just when he'd thought he'd put the whole Melly thing in perspective, she was churning him up again. Despite himself, he felt an extraordinary tenderness toward her, an instinct to protect her. From what? From the world? Or from herself? Whatever, he just hated to see her unhappy.

"But you don't *understand*," Melinda said helplessly.

He smiled quirkily. "I don't think anyone would find it easy to understand you, Melly," he said softly. "I don't think you quite understand yourself."

She slid off her stool. "I'd better go. I've got some shopping to do. Thanks for the lunch, Kyle."

"You're welcome." He stood, too, and they walked out of the hotel together. He heard himself asking, "How long will you be?"

"An hour or so, but—"

"I'll be returning about three-thirty, if you want a lift back. The car's in the lot behind the supermarket. We can sling the bike on the roof rack and put your groceries in the trunk."

Melinda shook her head. "Thanks, but I'll probably be finished before then."

"It'd still be quicker by car." Why in heaven's name was he pressing her? Why didn't he just let her go about her business without interference from him? That was what she wanted.

"I enjoy cycling," Melinda said independently.

He gave in. "Okay. Take care, Melly."

An hour later, loaded down with more shopping than she had originally intended because she had stacked the supermarket cart absently, forgetting she did not have the car, Melinda trudged back to where she had left her bike. With some difficulty she stowed her purchases in the double carrier on the back and the basket on the front. The bike was now heavy and difficult to maneuver. She wobbled precariously as she joined the line of traffic in the main street, hoping it would be quieter once she was on the Heron Valley road.

With her mind still turbulent with thoughts generated by her morning conversations with Mr. Cotham and Kyle, Melinda followed her route instinctively. Preoccupied, she did not see the broken bottle until too late to swerve around the shards littering the road. As the bicycle crunched over the broken glass she winced, then stopped to kick as much of the glass off the road as she could, before continuing on her way.

Nothing happened for half a mile and Melinda was beginning to think that she had been lucky, after all. Until, all at once, she was aware of a jerkiness in the front wheel, then pedaling became more difficult and within a few minutes she knew without doubt she had a puncture.

She dismounted. The back wheel looked ominously soft, too. The only thing she could do was walk and hope for a lift, or wait until someone came along.

Deciding she preferred to walk, she trudged on, wishing fervently she had not got so carried away with her shopping. Under pedal power it hadn't seemed so bad, but pushing the loaded bike was making her arms ache and her calves cramp.

She was nearly at the top of a long hill when at last she heard a car coming up behind. She turned around and was unsurprised to see Kyle grinning at her.

"It's not like you, Melly, to let a little hill defeat you," he chided, his eyes full of laughter now.

"I've got a puncture." She looked and sounded disgruntled, and her face was flushed.

Kyle pulled into the side of the road just ahead of her and got out. He took the loaded bicycle from her aching arms.

"Let's put your shopping in the trunk and the bike on the rack. When did it happen?"

"About half a mile back. A broken bottle. I kicked as much glass as I could into the ditch."

In moments her bags were stowed and her bike was lashed to the roof rack. As Kyle put the car into gear and swung out onto the road again, she said, "I guess it's not my day today. Thanks."

As they drove up to Riversham, Melinda was surprised to see a car she didn't recognize parked in front of it. "I wonder who that is. I'm not expecting anyone."

"A fan come to view the gold medal," suggested Kyle. "Or a customer to buy up your entire cellar."

Melinda wasn't amused. "Don't be facetious. It's a rental car by the look of it."

Kyle parked alongside the strange car, which was piled with luggage. As they got out, a woman ran out of the house, long blond hair flying. She flung herself into Melinda's arms, crying, "Oh, Melly, it is good to see you!"

"Caroline!" Melinda staggered, more from astonishment than the physical impact of the greeting. "What on earth are you doing here? I thought you weren't coming this year."

But momentarily Caroline's attention had been distracted as she became aware of Melinda's companion. Kyle was unlashing the bike, and Melinda's exclamation made him pause and stare at the other woman.

"Caroline Wells?" he murmured, recognition dawning.

"Kyle Macintosh," she said, more sure of her identification. "Well, what do you know?" She held out her hand to him.

Melinda, discarded for the moment, watched as their eyes met and Caroline's slow, sensuous smile worked a little magic on Kyle's expression. Irrationally she felt a deep resentment gradually displacing her spontaneous delight at seeing the friend she hadn't expected, and recognized with dismay that she was jealous.

Chapter Four

"What are you doing *here*, Caroline?" Melinda's repeated question eventually broke the eye contact between Caroline and Kyle.

Caroline, looking fabulous in a dress that advertised all her figure advantages at once, turned slowly. "I'm sorry I couldn't let you know I was coming, Melly, but I didn't know myself until the last minute that the schedule was going to be changed."

Melinda indicated with a look the luggage stacked in the back of the hired hatchback. "You haven't been home yet?" she asked, puzzled.

"It's a long story," said Caroline, casting a sideways glance at Kyle. "Why don't we have a cup of tea." She smiled invitingly as she added, "I was just about to put the kettle on and make myself one. Rocky said you probably wouldn't be long." Her voice sounded faintly North American after her years away in the United States.

"I'll be getting along," Kyle said. "Catch up with you later, Caroline."

Caroline was not to be denied. "Kyle, surely you can stay for a cup?" Her smile was persuasive. "Make him stay, Melinda. I want to know why *he's* back here after all these years."

Melinda felt obliged to say, "You can spare time for a cup of tea, Kyle, I'm sure."

Caroline's persuasive smile seemed to have worked already, because Kyle's protest sounded merely token, after all. Having removed Melinda's bicycle from his roof rack and her groceries from the trunk, he followed the two women into the kitchen.

Kyle deposited Melinda's bags of groceries on the kitchen counter, then sprawled in a chair, listening to their chatter and observing both women with interest. The small, sometimes volatile redhead and the cool, elegant, willowy blonde made a startling contrast, both in appearance and personality. Caroline had always been one to lavish attention on her appearance, and even as a teenager had cultivated an aura of glamour. It was inevitable that she should become a model. The difference between her and Melinda was that she knew she had sex appeal, and cultivated it, while Melly was unaware of how powerful her impact could be on a man.

Waiting for the kettle to boil, Melinda admired Caroline, who was perched on a stool at the breakfast bar, legs crossed at the knee and showing a tantalizing expanse of silk-clad thigh and a pair of very trim ankles in spike-heeled shoes. Kyle's eyes were making their own leisurely assessment, she noticed.

Caroline explained her unexpected appearance in husky tones. "I didn't think I had a hope in hell of coming back, yet again this year, but at the last minute they decided to do a series of shots in Australia instead of Mexico—"

"Hang on," interrupted Melinda. "Who did, and what shots? Don't forget we haven't heard a word from you for years, Caro. Are you still modeling?"

Caroline pouted contritely. "I'm a rotten correspondent, I know. I hate writing letters. And since I never could make the date, it always seemed a bit pointless writing to say so." She shrugged. "Well, it's like this, folks. Since we last met I've tried everything from model to air hostess to public relations consultant, and now I'm in business on my own."

"Are you still living in the States?" Melinda queried.

"Yes, I am."

"But why are you here now and not at your mother's?"

"Because she's on holiday in Bali. I hope you don't mind putting me up for a couple of extra days, Mel. Mom gets back on Sunday and I have to zoom off to Alice Springs on an assignment for *Vogue* a few days later." She paused to draw breath and smiled apologetically. "You are having a reunion this year? And it's still the same weekend?"

"Yes, of course we are. What's the assignment in Alice Springs?" Melinda asked. "What business are you in?"

"The rag trade, designing my own range of clothes. I've opened several very upscale boutiques in selected cities in the States, mostly in resorts where the rich holiday. I'm thinking of doing the same thing here. *Vogue* is doing a whole feature on me. Hence the cases full of gear. They're using local models. Knock wood, I think I've really arrived!" She paused and looked from one to the other. "Now, guys, tell me all about you. What are *you* doing here, Kyle? I heard you were big news in the hotel industry."

Kyle shrugged modestly and made a few comments about his new project. Melinda noticed that while he was speaking he received the rapt attention of Caroline's violet-blue eyes.

"Is your wife with you?" Caroline inquired casually.

"Gina and I are divorced," Kyle said abruptly.

Caroline murmured, "I'm so sorry," then covered the awkward moment by saying to Melinda, "and you're still not married, Mel?" She glanced at Kyle. "You know, we all expected Melly to be first to tie the knot."

"Melly's wedded to wine making," Kyle said. "She's too busy putting Riversham wines on the map." He urged Melinda to tell Caroline about the gold medal.

Compared with Caroline's exciting career, her own success didn't seem so fantastic to Melinda anymore. She felt gratified, however, when Caroline looked impressed and exclaimed, "Congratulations, Melly! That's fabulous. It must make it all seem worthwhile, a just reward at last for burying yourself here in the valley all these years."

Melinda didn't mind the faint pity. "It's gratifying to see Dad's hard work coming to fruition," she said.

A few moments later the back door slammed and they were interrupted by Matthew, who looked startled, then shy.

"Come in, Matthew," Melinda invited. "This is Caroline Wells, one of my old school friends."

Kyle said, "This is my son, Matthew. Matthew, say hello to Miss Wells."

Matthew murmured a shy hello and Caroline told him to please call her Caroline.

"I thought you weren't coming down here today?" Kyle said to his son.

Matthew looked anxiously at his father. "R-Robert rang up and asked me to come down. Th-there was a special job Rocky wanted us to do."

"Well, if you've finished it, I think we'd better be going now," Kyle said, rising. He held out his hand to Caroline. "Nice to see you again, Caro."

"Nice to see *you*," she purred, sliding her hand through his gracefully.

Melinda saw them off and then returned to the kitchen.

"Good-looking kid," Caroline remarked. "Like his father. How long has Kyle been divorced?"

"Only a few months. Gina has married again—a film director, I gather. Kyle doesn't say much. I got that from gossip columns and Rosa. You remember the housekeeper at Heronvale? She told me Matthew goes to stay with his mother sometimes, but she suspects he isn't really welcome. He's a bit of a problem child according to Rosa. Somewhat moody and given to tantrums. I think Kyle worries a lot about him, although he doesn't say much. Matthew spends most of his time over here, with Rocky's son, Robert. I think he's basically lonely, and he always seems nervous with his father. I don't think Kyle's unkind to him—far from it—but they don't seem to have a close relationship, which is a shame. I guess the divorce has a lot to do with it. It must have been pretty traumatic for Matthew.''

Caroline appeared to be listening, but Melinda sensed her attention was distracted. She examined her long scarlet nails, then looked up. ''I was wondering if you and he—''

''Don't be ridiculous!''

''What's ridiculous? You used to go around together.''

''Used to. Past tense.''

''But he's a free agent again and you're...'' She paused, and Melinda was certain she had been going to say ''on the shelf.''

''We had a teenage romance. At least, I was still a teenager. He was in his early twenties. We've nothing in common now.''

Caroline inclined her head thoughtfully. ''Wines and hotels—they're not so far removed from each other. I'd say there's a definite connection.''

''As far as I'm concerned only a business one. Kyle's going to order some Riversham wines.''

Reluctant to pursue this line of conversation, Melinda ran her fingers through her tousled locks. ''I feel a mess. I think I'll have a shower and change before I cook dinner. I won't be long. Make yourself at home, won't you, Caro?''

Under the shower, letting the stinging needles of first hot then cold water revitalize her body, which was already developing mild aches from using muscles she hadn't exercised for a while, Melinda suddenly found herself thinking of the men she might have married over the past ten years. She hadn't turned them down just because she hadn't wanted to leave the valley; she had, after all, very nearly become engaged to Brook Longmuir, who ran one of the biggest vineyards in the valley. But although that and other relationships had started off well, they had eventually petered out. There had always been something vital missing, some spark that she looked for and didn't find. It must be a lack in her, she had often felt.

Melinda stepped out of the shower and toweled herself vigorously, turning her thoughts to what she would cook for dinner. And tonight she would not give Kyle one single thought, not one. She would gossip with Caroline and make sure they talked about every subject under the sun except Kyle Macintosh. She was not going to let him dominate her thoughts. This advice to herself continued as she dressed in comfortable navy slacks and a loose-fitting mauve sweater.

Over dinner Melinda told Caroline what she knew of the others. "Rose was on a modeling assignment in Italy when she wrote, but she was definite she'd be able to make it. Sylvana is combining the reunion with a business trip. The fine arts auctioneer she works for in London has a branch in Melbourne. And Katherine never has any problem taking time off from her medical practice. She moved to London for a couple of years, but she's back in Sydney now.''

"What about Mary Brabich?"

"She can't come. She's on an archaeological dig in North Africa."

"God! The last time I heard, it was Patagonia or somewhere equally remote."

Melinda unpinned the postcards from the bulletin board and handed them to Caroline to read while she served the dessert.

After coffee Melinda was not surprised when Caroline yawned and decided to retire early. She had been traveling nonstop for two days before she'd arrived at Riversham.

Melinda went to bed early herself, but she could not sleep. The ultimate fate of Jarrahwood had been pushed into the background with Caroline's arrival, but now the hopelessness of the cause returned to plague her. Was it merely selfishness, as Kyle had implied, wanting to keep the property as it was, an indulgence just for her own pleasure? Or was it environmentally important? As soon as she could, she decided, she would seek an expert opinion.

The next day Melinda was scheduled to be tied up all day seeing customers and conducting a wine tasting for them, and when she apologized, Caroline dismissed her apology graciously.

"No worries! I'll spend a quiet day recovering from jet lag. I might get out of your way and go explore old haunts. Unless there's anything I can do to help?"

"No, nothing," said Melinda. "Dot Nankervis comes in today to unravel my week's muddle. You remember Dot and her brothers?"

"Do I ever! Dot used to fight all their battles for them. No kids ever had a more loyal older sister. I suppose she mothers you, too, now?"

Melinda laughed. "She tries to." Then she offered, "If you want to borrow the bike, feel free. I had a puncture yesterday, but Rocky's fixed it."

"Thanks for the offer, but I don't think I have the energy for more strenuous exercise today. Don't worry about lunch for me. I might drive into Heronbush and mosey around a bit."

Melinda's day flew. She paused only briefly for a snack at lunchtime and a chat with Dot. At five o'clock she farewelled her visitors with a sigh of relief, and with the gratification of some firm orders for Riversham wines from customers who had not patronized her winery before.

In the kitchen she made herself a cup of tea and skimmed through the usual cryptic notes left by Dot. She was pinning the one concerning food supplies required for the weekend to her kitchen bulletin board when Caroline came in looking windblown and healthily flushed.

"Did you have a good day?" Melinda asked.

"Terrific."

"Did you go into Heronbush?"

"I did. I had lunch at the Heronbush Hotel. Guess who with."

"An old flame?"

"No! Kyle Macintosh. I bumped into him in the street."

Just as she had herself a few days ago, Melinda thought, surprised at how resentful she felt about Caroline's repeating the event.

"He invited us to dinner at his place tonight," said Caroline, obviously pleased. "I said all right. It is, isn't it? You're not doing anything else?"

Melinda wondered if Caroline was hoping she was. "No," she said quickly. "But I'm a bit tired. It's been a hectic day. But you go, Caro."

Caroline looked doubtful. "Are you sure? I said I'd phone if it wasn't okay."

"I'll let Rosa know," Melinda offered.

Caroline went off to shower and change while Melinda phoned Heronvale.

Rosa said, "Matthew will be disappointed. He is already looking forward to it." She chuckled. "He told me I have to make the best Italian meal in the world for you. It is a special occasion for him."

Melinda was touched. "Tell him I'm sorry, Rosa. Maybe some other time." But she didn't think Kyle would ever invite her alone. In fact, she hoped he wouldn't. It seemed to be getting harder and harder to cope with him in her mind, never mind in the flesh.

A few minutes later the phone rang. It was Matthew. He didn't beat about the bush.

"Melly, why aren't you coming to dinner tonight?"

Melinda drew in a deep breath. "Didn't Rosa tell you? I've had a busy day and I'm rather tired. I've got visitors coming for the weekend and I need an early night."

"You have to eat," he argued.

Melinda couldn't help laughing. "I plan to have a quick snack and go to bed. I need my beauty sleep, Matthew."

"You do not! You're already beautiful."

"Thank you. You're welcome at my place anytime."

"Please, Melly," he pleaded. "Please come. I want to show you things, Melly. I've been asking Dad for *ages* to invite you, but he never has. He said Nonna couldn't have visitors because she was still sad about Granddad, but she must be all right now or he wouldn't have asked you tonight. Please come."

The plaintive note in Matthew's voice was impossible to ignore. "All right," she said. "But if I fall asleep and snore, your grandmother will be insulted and it'll be your fault."

Matthew laughed. "She'll be insulted if you don't come. Promise you will?"

Melinda gave a resigned sigh. "Yes, I promise. You're a very persuasive young man."

Matthew whooped with delight. "I'll tell Rosa. See you!"

Melinda met Caroline coming out of the bathroom. "I'm coming after all," she told her ruefully. "Matthew was just on the phone, and it seems I can't say no to small boys."

"So long as you can to big ones!" joked Caroline, and Melinda wasn't sure whether she looked pleased or disappointed at not having Kyle to herself this evening, after all.

When, at seven-thirty, Melinda parked the car outside the old house at Heronvale with its wide, vine-clad verandas and rambling garden, she felt a strong pang of nostalgia. She'd been up here only once briefly since Kyle had come back, after the funeral. Tonight her memories of years gone by, of birthday parties when they'd all been small, of barbecues when they were older, of teenage love, were poignantly alive.

Matthew dashed out of the house to greet them. He clutched Melinda's hand with relief in his dark, intense eyes, as though he'd been afraid she might break her promise, after all. She wondered if broken promises had been a regular part of his life. In divorce it was often the children who suffered most.

Rosa appeared and warmly hugged Caroline, whom she remembered well. As they went inside, Matthew grinned up at Melinda. "I'm so glad you came." Then he said mischievously, "Rosa, she make-a da pasta and da zuppa and da zabaglione and if you no come-a to eat-a da food, she have to feed-a it all to the chooks!"

Melinda, convulsed with laughter, nevertheless scolded, "Shh! You shouldn't mock Rosa like that. It's very unkind. She speaks English as well as you do even if she still does have an accent." Fortunately the housekeeper was a few paces ahead, chatting to Caroline, and didn't hear.

Matthew, encouraged by Melinda's mirth, started showing off. He gave an impersonation of his grandmother, catching her imperious tone exactly.

Stifling her giggles, Melinda tried to sound stern. "Matthew! Stop it—they'll hear you!"

There was no stopping him now and he went on to mimic his father, so accurately that Melinda caught her breath. She rumpled his dark hair, reluctant to

squash his high spirits too much. "If you don't behave yourself, I'll go home again."

He kept a tight grip on her hand. "No! I won't let
you."

Perhaps he would eventually become an actor like
his mother, Melinda thought. Wanting to be a vigneron was more than likely to prove a passing ambition.
He was enthusiastic probably only because he was
staying in the valley and vineyards were a novelty to
him.

Kyle's mother was waiting in the drawing room. Her
black silk dress was austere and contrasted starkly with
her white hair. She was not tall, but very slender and
very aristocratic looking. Kyle was not there.

"Good evening, Mrs. Macintosh." Melinda felt, as
she always had, that the name seemed inappropriate
for this regal Italian lady.

Caroline also murmured a greeting.

"Melinda...lovely to see you. And Caroline."
Angelina Macintosh spoke softly, with a musical ca-
dence in her voice. The slight austerity of her appearance vanished in a warm smile that did not, however,
completely hide the sadness that lurked in her dark
olive eyes, the grieving for Kyle's father. She kissed
them lightly on the cheeks.

"Do sit down. Kyle won't be long," said Angelina.
"He is on the telephone to Sydney. You would like a
drink?" Her voice, despite a lifetime living in Australia, still had a distinct Italian accent, and when Rosa
came in with a tray of appetizers it was obvious from
their exchanges that Angelina had never lost fluency
in her native tongue. Rosa beamed at the two visitors.
She was an unmarried cousin of Angelina's who had

come to keep house for the family some fifteen years ago.

Angelina offered sherry to her guests. As Melinda was taking a crystal glass from the silver tray, Kyle came in. She could not help a swift intake of breath. In the Italianate surroundings he suddenly looked more Latin and as austerely aristocratic as his mother. In comparison with her small stature, he also seemed taller and more physically dominant than ever.

"My apologies, ladies," he said. "I was on the telephone when you arrived. Ah, good, you already have a drink." He offered a dish of appetizers and olives. In a crisp white shirt and navy blue trousers, he looked smart but casual. Expensively casual, Melinda thought, noting the close fit of the trousers on his slim hips, the quality of the shirt.

Melinda had never felt completely comfortable with Kyle's mother, but the reason she did not feel at ease now was as much Kyle's fault as his mother's. Although she endeavored not to, she kept meeting his eyes and feeling uneasy because she was unable to read the expression in them.

The dinner was a superb example of Rosa's culinary skills and there was very little left for the hens. Which, Melinda remarked in a low voice to Matthew at her side, should please Rosa.

He whispered, "But not the hens!" and broke into a loud peal of laughter that earned him a sharp rebuke from his father. Matthew's ebullience instantly evaporated and he looked sullen—the moodiness Rosa had spoken about, Melinda realized.

After dinner they returned to the drawing room. Rosa brought in coffee, and as soon as he noticed she had finished hers, Matthew begged Melinda to go with him to look at his Lego constructions and his drawings.

"Time you were in bed, young man," Kyle said.

Matthew looked rebellious, so Melinda interceded. "Ten minutes, Kyle?"

He hesitated, but finally agreed with a nod, and Melinda left them, dragged away eagerly by Matthew.

He whispered, "Thanks, Melinda. You sure can twist Dad around your little finger, can't you?" His eyes were wide with admiration.

"I most certainly cannot. Your father just didn't want a scene. Count yourself lucky, young man."

Matthew gave her the kind of unfathomable look that his father sometimes bestowed on her.

The ten minutes stretched to fifteen as Matthew showed Melinda not only his complicated Lego constructions but also his scrapbooks and his cassette collection, all of which, she suspected, was a ploy to spin out the time so that he would not have to go to bed yet.

Finally Melinda, glancing at her watch, said, "I reckon it's time you cleaned your teeth and went to bed, Matt, don't you? Before your dad catches you out. We've had twenty minutes already."

He pulled a face. "Have we? It doesn't seem that long." He looked at her for a moment, then astonished her by saying soulfully, "Will you tuck me in?"

Melinda was startled. "Well, of course I will, darling," she said. Most boys of his age would scorn being tucked in, but if Matthew wanted her to, she was happy to oblige.

To her astonishment and intense embarrassment, he suddenly flung his arms around her and cried hoarsely, "I wish you were my mother! I don't want to go back to Sydney. I want to come and live with you."

Melinda was not sure how to handle a situation so delicate. She hugged him tightly and tried to make light of it. "Oh, Matt, we all wish things like that sometimes, especially when our own mothers won't let us do what we want."

He mumbled into her shoulder, "I have to go and stay with her but I hate it! I know she doesn't really want me there. I'm just a nuisance. She says she's going to take me out, to a film or something, and she never does. She's always got a script to read or someone to see, or somewhere to go where I can't go, too. Sometimes I have to stay home in their flat by myself. Greg's even worse. He teases, or just ignores me. He doesn't like kids, I heard him say so. Dad was talking to her on the phone tonight and they were having a row. I could tell it was about me. I know they wish I'd never been born—" He broke off and wriggled free, to stand looking guiltily over Melinda's shoulder.

Melinda turned around. Kyle was standing in the doorway. His grim expression suggested that he had probably heard everything said in the past minute or two. Melinda got up, impulsively put her arm around Matthew's shoulders and held him protectively against her side. Still trying for lightness, she said, "Don't shoot! We give up! The prisoner's going back to his cell forthwith." She swung Matthew into a frog-march position and faced him toward the door. "If you want me to stay to say good-night, bathroom at the double, Matthew Macintosh. One-two, one-two...."

Kyle stood aside to let his son bolt through. There was no smile on the tightly compressed lips, yet he didn't seem to be angry.

Melinda yawned. "I'm about ready for bed myself. Do you mind if I go as soon as I've said good-night to Matthew? There's no need for me to drag Caroline away if you'll drive her home later."

"She's probably as tired as you."

Maybe, Melinda thought, but I bet she won't turn down the chance of being alone with you. She moved to the door, which his large frame had filled again, but he did not stand aside to let her through as he had for his son. Instead, he pulled her into his arms and laid his cheek against her hair with an almost inaudible groan. Although there was emotional intensity between them, it wasn't sensual.

Melinda felt a sudden wave of compassion for Matthew and his father. She had the feeling that if she said, "Tell me about it..." Kyle would unburden himself, but it was neither the time nor the place. Besides, what advice could she offer? What comfort, even?

"I'm sorry, Kyle," she said. "It must be tough for you, but I'm sure things will turn out better, given time. You and Matthew will come to terms with it in time." It wasn't much of a consolation, but words were not coming easily to her right then.

He didn't reply, and Matthew's return, together with the appearance of Rosa to check on him, forced them apart hastily. Kyle said good-night to his son rather brusquely and went back to the living room. Melinda tucked Matthew into bed and kissed him. She felt awkward and inexperienced, yet extraordinarily tender toward the boy. It was ironic, she thought, that she had a great deal in common with Kyle's son, but between her and Kyle there was an unbridgeable gulf.

"I bet you'll sleep like a log tonight," she said.

As she turned to go, he called her back. "Melly..."

"Yes?"

"When Dad goes back to Sydney...do you reckon I could stay behind?"

Melinda sat on the edge of the bed, disturbed. "I don't think your father would like that, Matt."

His small, serious face was very determined. "I don't care. I hate Sydney. I hate having to go and stay with Mommy and Greg. It's so boring up there. I haven't got any friends. Here I've got Robert and I could go to the same school he does, and work for Rocky. Nonna says one day I could take over Heron-vale."

Melinda drew in a sharp breath. Kyle had evidently not told the child he wanted his mother to sell the property. "Well, that's looking a long way ahead."

"Only about ten years. Nonna will be pretty old by then, and she'll need someone to take care of everything," the child said seriously.

"Have you talked to your father about this?" Melinda asked. "Have you asked your grandmother if she could put up with having you?" She did not laugh. Matthew was in deadly earnest.

He grinned appealingly. "No. I want you to do that for me, Melly—*please*. You talk to Dad. He'll listen to you. He told Nonna you're the most intelligent woman he's come across in a month of Sundays."

Melinda was warmed by the unexpected compliment so ingenuously relayed by Matthew, who went on eagerly, "You can twist his arm. I reckon he'll be relieved, really. I'm just a pain in the neck to him. He has to keep remembering to be kind to me and he's not terribly good at it."

"Matthew!"

"It's true. I'm just a millstone around their necks."

"Who said that?" Melinda inquired sharply.

He shrugged. "Oh, Greg, I think."

"About you?" Melinda was horrified.

"I suppose so. He and Mom were arguing as usual. Just like she used to argue with Dad. She's very argumentative."

Melinda was at a loss. And any minute now, Kyle was going to come looking for her. "Matthew, I'd better go," she said. "It's time your light was out."

"You'll ask Dad?" he asked anxiously.

"Yes, all right. I'll talk to him, but I won't promise to try and persuade him. I don't think he'll agree to it, Matthew, and I'm not sure your grandmother would, either."

He answered confidently, "She would. She's lonely now that Granddad's dead. Italian grandmothers always like to spoil their grandchildren. And Rosa likes anyone with a big appetite."

"You little monster!" Melinda chided. "Go to sleep, and we'll talk about it later." She dropped a kiss on his forehead, then switched off the light beside the bed and moved to the doorway. Matthew called her again.

"Now what?"

"Thanks, Melly. I think you're ace."

Melinda didn't feel ace. She felt alarmed. What on earth was Kyle going to say? He probably wouldn't take very kindly to her having been engaged as mediator for his son. She would have to think very carefully about how she approached him.

Melinda was now more anxious than ever to leave early. She apologized to Angelina and waited for Kyle to invite Caroline to stay a little longer. But he didn't. Melinda remembered that Matthew had said he'd been talking to, perhaps even arguing with, his ex-wife, so she concluded that he was not in the mood for chatting up Caroline.

If Caroline was disappointed she concealed it well. She yawned and said, "I'm more than a little weary myself." She turned to Mrs. Macintosh. "Thank you for a wonderful meal. It was marvelous to see you again." Her smile encompassed Kyle also.

Melinda said her thanks and Kyle escorted them out to the car. It was with a sense of relief that Melinda coasted down the long, poplar-lined driveway and onto the road.

"Kyle was an old sobersides tonight, wasn't he?" Caroline commented.

"He did seem a bit preoccupied," agreed Melinda. She didn't mention the phone call from Gina. So far as she was concerned, that was confidential.

They both went straight to bed, but despite her tiredness Melinda was troubled far into the night by her conversation with Matthew, and more than a little disconcerted by her emotional encounter with Kyle in Matthew's bedroom. Somehow, despite herself, or perhaps just because of her concern for Matthew, she seemed to be getting more involved with them than was wise.

Chapter Five

Next morning, yawning as she spooned breakfast cereal into a bowl, Melinda wondered when she was ever going to get a good night's sleep again. Dribbling milk over her muesli and adding yogurt, she contemplated her problems. Jarrahwood seemed to be doomed, and all she could do about Matthew was talk to Kyle, an ordeal she didn't relish. He was bound to resent her interference.

"Oh, hell," she complained to the milk jug. "Why did I have to get involved?"

"If you've started talking to yourself, it's time you stopped living alone." Caroline lounged in the kitchen doorway, a blue satin robe clutched around her.

Melinda was startled. "Sorry. I do tend to think aloud sometimes."

Caroline strolled in and perched on a stool. She helped herself to cereal, and coffee from the pot Melinda had just made, and asked, "Anything you want me to do today? Can I go shopping for you? Do you need anything for the weekend?"

"I have to go to Heronbush, so why don't we both go?" Melinda suggested. "That'll leave the house clear for Dot for an hour or two. She hates people under her feet when she's vacuuming."

"What time do you expect the others tomorrow?" Caroline asked.

"Midmorning. Certainly in time for lunch." Which meant, she was thinking, that unless she could find time to plead Matthew's case with Kyle this afternoon, she would not have a chance until after the weekend.

Lingering over a second cup of coffee with Caroline, Melinda wrote out her shopping list and by the time Dot Nankervis arrived, they were ready to leave for Heronbush.

They finished the shopping quickly, window-shopped for a while, then had coffee to while away another hour because Melinda said Dot would be put out if they returned too soon. When they arrived back at Riversham, Dot had gone, the house was sparkling and there was a sheaf of scrawled notes on the counter, which Caroline laughingly deciphered and read aloud as Melinda swiftly prepared a quick lunch of soup and salad-filled pita bread.

"'Here are your phone messages,'" Caroline read out in a fair imitation of Dot's brisk accent. "'Mr. Brace of Brace Brothers Wine Merchants wants you to call him back urgently. Katherine might be late but please keep her some lunch as she won't have had any. Your rubber stamp is ready. When can rep from Ferguson Fertilizers call? *Winegrower* magazine wants to interview you about gold medal'—with three exclamation marks!'' Caroline looked up at Melinda. "I suppose you'll have all the wine writers wanting to interview you now you're famous.''

The prospect of publicity of the personal kind made Melinda apprehensive. "I'm not exactly famous.''

"Give it time,'' said Caroline. "Oh, here's another message. Katherine won't be late, after all, and she's bringing the others.''

After lunch Caroline admitted to delayed jet lag and retired to her room. Melinda, although feeling a little jaded herself, couldn't afford the luxury of catching up on lost sleep. She had promised to see Gianni about delivery of the new French oak casks they would be needing, and to check their bottle supplies. There had been a mistake in the last consignment. "And I'd better tell Rocky about the fertilizer people,'' she muttered to herself as she hurried down to the winery.

Her tasks gave her no opportunity to phone Kyle about Matthew that afternoon. She brooded uneasily over what she would say to him when she did broach the subject. She was sure Kyle would be reluctant to let the boy stay with his grandmother. Kyle was hoping to persuade his mother to sell Heronvale.

Next morning Melinda was on the phone when a big green car swung around the house and stopped just out of her line of vision through the office window. She had glimpsed its occupants, so she quickly wound up her conversation, dropped the receiver on the rest and ran to greet her friends. Caroline was ahead of her, and shrieks of delighted surprise were echoing around the old homestead.

For a few moments there was pandemonium as they hugged and kissed each other. Then they trooped after Melinda into the house and she showed them their rooms.

"Same ones as always," Melinda directed, "unless you want to swap. Coffee in five minutes," she added, leaving them to settle in.

At morning tea, sprawled on loungers in the sun room, the five women regarded each other speculatively. Melinda saw that despite the initial greetings of "You haven't changed a bit," they all had, subtly.

As usual at their reunions, each of the five friends gave a brief résumé of what had been happening since their last reunion. When Melinda told them about the gold medal, there were cries of congratulation, and wild speculations on the direction her future might now take.

After lunch, still in high spirits, and reminiscing about when they'd all lived in the valley, they persuaded Melinda to take them to visit the old primary school where they'd all commenced their education. It was unused now and Melinda had expected to find it locked, but a side door wasn't, so they went in and spent a nostalgic half hour bombarding each other with memories. Afterward, they couldn't resist trying out the old swings and parallel bars, until suddenly Sylvana yelled, "Watch out! Here comes old Possum-face!"

Guiltily they all stopped fooling around as though their former headmaster, rudely nicknamed Possum-face, had indeed caught them red-handed doing something they shouldn't. But it wasn't the much-feared but much-revered head teacher of their day striding across the weed-ridden school yard. It was Kyle.

"What on earth . . . ?" He looked from one to the other of the flushed and sheepish faces, and burst out laughing. "I thought some hooligans were vandalizing the place."

Rose, eyeing Kyle with interest and open admiration, said mockingly, "You haven't changed a bit, Kyle Macintosh. Of course, you always were disgustingly good-looking."

Kyle joined in their lighthearted banter for a few minutes, then said he must be on his way. Rose glanced at Melinda and ventured hopefully, "Why don't we invite Kyle to have dinner with us tonight?" She gave him a provocative look. "Are you game? Can you handle five women at once?"

Kyle laughed. "I thought tonight was strictly a hen party. I believe I'm invited over for coffee tomorrow morning."

"You can come then, too," said Rose enthusiastically. "But as we haven't seen you for so long..." She looked at the others for support. "What do you think, girls?"

Caroline drawled, "Yes, do come, Kyle."

Katherine and Sylvana pressed him, too, and all looked for final approval from Melinda. Kyle also caught Melinda's eye. "I don't want to intrude," he said.

"Of course you're welcome." Their eyes held for a moment and Melinda felt suddenly possessive, reluctant to share him with the others.

* * *

That evening Melinda was helping Rose with the zipper on a very slinky blue silk garment that showed to advantage every curve in her friend's slender but shapely figure when Kyle arrived. Dot's voice floated along the passage as she let him in.

"Hello, Kyle. You're a brave man dining with five women!"

Kyle's warm laughter preceded his reply. "A lucky man, Dot. Besides, there's safety in numbers, isn't there?"

"I dunno," said Dot seriously. "Not when they're all as stunning as this lot."

Rose whispered, "He's developed a very sexy voice." She rolled her eyes. "And you say he's unattached at the moment?"

"So far as I know."

Rose, zipped up, left, and Melinda finished her own dressing. For tonight she had chosen black ski pants and a soft apricot cashmere sweater that enhanced her coloring.

The others were already chatting to Kyle when Melinda emerged. Initially there was a bit of teasing and half-serious flirtation as her friends competed for Kyle's attention, but he shared himself equally and was careful, Melinda noticed, not to monopolize anyone. He also adroitly sidestepped oblique questions about Gina, his divorce and his current love life. Melinda wondered if what he'd said to her about it in an unguarded moment was true. Kyle without female company was hard to imagine. Several times when he wasn't looking her way, Melinda studied his profile, wondering what he was thinking, but Kyle's expression, behind the nods and smiles, was as inscrutable as ever.

Dot had gone, the dishwasher had finished its cycle and Melinda was about to brew another pot of coffee when Kyle joined her in the kitchen, brandishing an empty bottle. He shouted over the din of the coffee grinder, "You don't happen to have another bottle of Tia Maria, do you?"

"Oh, yes. I forgot that one was nearly empty. It's Rose and Sylvana's favorite liqueur, and I did remember to buy a bottle yesterday. I think I shoved it in the pantry cupboard. On the bottom shelf." She was aware of his eyes regarding her rather intently as she spoke, and the power those enigmatic brown depths had to unnerve her was never more potent.

While he rummaged in the cupboard for the liqueur, Melinda turned away to switch off the grinder. She was tipping the grounds into the filter when she tingled at a presence behind her, and then shivered deliciously at the light touch of fingertips on the nape of her neck.

"Kyle..." She spilled some coffee as she half turned to shake off his hand while trying to laugh. "What are you doing?"

For answer he leaned forward and brushed his lips against her temple. "Just saying thanks for a pleasant evening, while I have you alone."

"I'm glad you're enjoying it." Her heart was racing out of control.

"Immensely. Who wouldn't, surrounded by five beautiful women?"

"Have you managed to make dates with them all, without the others knowing?" Regrettably, she sounded sarcastic while meaning merely to tease.

"Of course!" he said, straight-faced. He put the bottle of Tia Maria on the counter, then leaned back on the edge of it, arms folded, almost challenging her. "All except you, of course." A wave of dark hair had slipped across his forehead, and the black sweater and gray flannels emphasized his powerful physique.

"Don't ask me," she said lightly. "I don't like being one of many."

With a sudden smooth movement he glided to her like a black panther pouncing, and as he grasped her bare upper arms, drawing her against him, a gasp escaped her lips. Only this was no savage predator holding her captive, this was a man with a glint in his eye that suggested seduction, not slaughter. Melinda's stomach muscles twisted and clenched in an alarming but not unpleasant way.

Voices and laughter from the living room seemed to recede into the distance. After a moment Melinda said shakily, "Why don't you go and pour the girls another Tia Maria, hand around the Turkish delight and let me make the coffee?"

Kyle answered in a gravelly undertone. "Any man who made you one of many would need his head examined," he murmured before he let her go and moved away.

Melinda finished filling the filter, placed it firmly in the container and switched it on. There was a moment of complete silence; even the sounds from the living room were briefly muted, while Kyle rolled the bottle of liqueur in his hands and Melinda felt as though she was in a state of suspended animation. The strong emotional current that flowed between them seemed to envelop her in an aura of warmth that made her tingle, as though warm fingers stroked her skin. The coffeemaker spluttered rudely and broke the spell.

Kyle put the bottle of liqueur down again on the counter. His hand came up and tilted her chin, making her look at him. The sensual power in his eyes made her whole body boneless.

She wrenched her face away. "Don't, Kyle."

Strong hands gripped her shoulders and he jerked her into his arms and matched his mouth firmly to hers. Tightening his arms around her, he used the support of the counter behind him to draw her hard between his thighs, flexing his leg muscles to imprison her there. The force of his kiss strained her head back and although she tried to resist, some power beyond herself softened her mouth and drew a pleasurable gasp from her parted lips.

He released her for a moment and raised his head to look at her. His eyes smoldered with a more open desire than she'd ever seen there before. There was no playful teasing in his manner now. His cards were on the table. And she was a fool to have let him take even that much advantage of her.

He slid his hand across her shoulder and nape up into her hair. "God, Melly, have you any idea what you're doing to me?" He moved closer, imprisoning her between his body and the counter now, and his lips were about to capture hers again when he abruptly dropped his hands to his sides. Melinda, sensing why, drew back guiltily and glanced around. Caroline was standing in the doorway, pretending to look shocked.

"I thought you must have gone to Heronbush to buy the Tia Maria," she drawled, her eyes flicking from one to the other with interest.

"It did take a bit of finding," Kyle answered with remarkable aplomb. "Melly couldn't remember where she'd put it." He tossed the bottle from one hand to the other and marched off to the living room.

"Do you want a hand with the coffee?" Caroline asked.

Warm color had flooded Melinda's face. "No—no, thanks. It's nearly ready. I won't be a minute."

Caroline lifted an eyebrow and gave her an amused look. Without commenting, she followed Kyle.

Next morning the incident still rankled with Melinda because there had been no chance last night to explain to Caroline that she mustn't jump to any conclusions about what she had seen and to appeal to her not to tell the others. Just how she was going to explain being in Kyle's arms she wasn't sure, so as soon as she was up she called Polly and took the dog for a walk before instead of after breakfast.

Polly seemed disinclined to follow the usual bush track and set off toward the river, nose to the ground as though following a compelling scent. Melinda followed, not caring which direction they went. She still felt angry with Kyle. He might have guessed someone would come in. Surely he realized it would be embarrassing for her?

She was just working herself into a nice old lather about it, and rehearsing a few well-chosen words to fling at him next time she saw him, when pounding steps behind her made her turn. She had forgotten that

Kyle went jogging along the riverbank in the mornings. Rufus greeted her first with paws on her chest and wagging tail, then charged off after Polly, who was barking joyously.

Kyle stopped, regarding Melinda with surprise. "Don't tell me you've decided to take up jogging, too?"

"No." The words for even a casual greeting were refusing to form in her brain. Even the heated words she had intended to throw at him seemed to have evaporated.

"I thought you usually took your walk in the bush."

"Polly decided to come this way for a change."

He raised a skeptical eyebrow and Melinda guessed he was wondering if she'd come on purpose to run into him. Well, let him put what construction he liked on it. It wasn't going to get him anywhere. She supposed it would have been an idea if she'd thought of it. Maybe she should thank Polly for engineering it. After all, she needed to see Kyle alone about Matthew and now might be as good an opportunity as any. But somehow she couldn't bring herself to broach the subject. Scantily clad in tank top and blue satin running shorts, he exuded too much raw masculinity, and the muscular strength of his arms, chest and legs—formerly only hinted at by clothing—was too disturbing. Besides, in the mood she was in, angry with him over last night, rational discussion about Matthew was out of the question.

"Don't let me hold you up," she said hastily. "You might catch a chill."

There was a tease in his eyes. "And vindicate your opinion of jogging."

"I must get back." He was blocking the path, but she could hardly push past him.

To her relief, he stood aside. "Great party last night," he murmured as she passed him. "Enjoy the rest of your reunion. I won't come for coffee this morning."

"Just as you like."

"Picnic today, is it?"

"Yes. Dinner out tonight. They go home tomorrow." She wanted to go, but he seemed to be intent on delaying her, as though he had something he wanted to say but wasn't sure how to phrase it. If it was an apology for embarrassing her in front of Caroline, she didn't want to hear it. That would only embarrass her more. "They'll be wanting breakfast," she said. "See you later, Kyle."

"Yeah, sure."

She hurried away, her composure ripped to shreds once more. She wished he'd hurry up and go home— to Sydney. She quickened her pace and almost broke into a run, as though the homestead offered sanctuary. But it didn't, not from her thoughts. Or from Caroline's curiosity.

Caroline was in the kitchen making coffee, but the others weren't up yet. She said nothing, and Melinda foolishly launched into a highly implausible explanation about stumbling and nearly dropping the bottle of Tia Maria, while Caroline just smiled.

Finally Caroline said, "Melly, you don't have to explain. If there's something between you two that's at a delicate stage, you don't have to talk about it."

"There's nothing," Melinda insisted.

Caroline asked bluntly, "Do you want there to be, Melly? Are you falling in love with him all over again?"

Melinda stared at her. It was the question she had avoided putting to herself. "No, of course not." She wanted to add, "All I know is, it's hell having him back in the valley."

Caroline frowned. "He's just trying to take advantage of your previous relationship to play around a little, is that it?"

Was that it? Melinda was only too well aware that Caroline had probably hit the nail on the head. Nevertheless, she said, "Most men like to flirt, don't they?"

Caroline shrugged. "Curse them!" She laughed, then said speculatively, "Maybe he's thinking of settling back in the valley."

Melinda scorned the suggestion. "Kyle! Hardly. He has a flourishing business empire. He's well-known in all the right circles. He loves the bright lights, the glamour, the pace of city life. He couldn't wait to get away from the valley, and he's chomping at the bit now. He'll be off again the minute he's settled things at Heronvale. He's still here now only because he's trying to persuade his mother to sell."

"Maybe he'll also try to persuade you to go with him this time."

Melinda shook her head, suddenly unable to answer, and Caroline said, "You are still in love with him, aren't you?"

Melinda covered her face with her hands. "No!"

"Why didn't you go with him before?" Caroline asked.

"I—I couldn't. I was needed here...."

"Not as much as you pretend. Your parents were both fit then."

Melinda poured herself a cup of coffee. "I know. But I just didn't want to leave the valley. I'm a valley person, Caro. Kyle isn't."

"You'd soon have got used to a new life-style. Country people can get used to living in cities, you know, and vice versa."

"Some can, but it doesn't always work. Roots go much deeper for some people than others. Sometimes when people try to change themselves, they make everyone unhappy. Kyle wouldn't have been happy staying in the valley."

"But if you love someone..." Caroline persisted, unconvinced.

"If you love someone," Melinda said softly, "you don't do something that may ultimately bring that person unhappiness. Sometimes you have to let them go their way and you go yours."

"There is such a thing as compromise."

"It doesn't always work," Melinda answered slowly. "You hear all too often of women leaving their husbands because they can't cope with a changed life-style that sometimes comes with career success, that maybe they couldn't have foreseen in the beginning. Look at Katherine. She couldn't take being a politician's wife. I'd have been crazy to put myself in that sort of position, knowing from the start it was a risk."

"I suppose you're right," murmured Caroline doubtfully. "But while you're still in love with Kyle you're not going to fall for anyone else."

"I'm not in love with Kyle now," Melinda said emphatically. "I'm talking about years ago."

Their conversation was, mercifully for Melinda, cut short when Katherine strolled into the kitchen, gasping for orange juice, shortly followed by Rose and Sylvana.

Later in the morning Dot arrived with a ready-packed picnic hamper, and they all piled into Melinda's car and drove off to a picnic spot by the river.

After feasting on Dot's luscious fare and drinking the chilled white wine Melinda had provided, they spent a lazy afternoon strolling along the riverbank, talking, talking, talking.... It was always like that at reunion weekends, as though they couldn't stop because there was so much to cram into the time. Although she joined in, Melinda's mind was forever slipping away into thoughts of Kyle.

On their return to Riversham, Melinda took them on a tour of the winery, proudly showing them, among other new equipment, her rotating fermentor for red wines and the modern tank press that extracted the juice from the grapes, crushing them gently so that the seeds were not shattered, to avoid any bitterness in the wine. Gianni, who accompanied them, provided the technical information.

"A far cry from treading the grapes!" Rose laughed. "Remember the wine festivals we used to have? They were fun, weren't they?"

"They still are," said Melinda, "but we don't even tread grapes at festivals anymore." She briefly closed her eyes. There was one festival she remembered vividly because she'd trodden grapes with Kyle, and they'd got so much juice over them that they'd hosed each other down amid gales of laughter. She remembered eating purple Cornichons with Kyle, and Kyle laughingly kissing the grape juice off her lips.... Oh, damn, she thought, why do I keep resurrecting a teenage infatuation that was merely my first real love affair?

She took a deep breath and, as they walked past the fermentation tanks, forced herself to concentrate on summarizing the whole wine-making process again for her friends. "So that's it—the grapes are fed down into the crusher back there, then the juice goes into the fermentation tanks and finally the new wine is clarified and some is matured in oak barrels before bottling, while the lighter red wines and the whites are bottled without further maturation. We ought to have the reunion one year when it's all happening. It's a bit dull now with everything empty. Let's go and look at the cellars."

They inspected the cool, underground cellars that smelled of damp earth, and then Melinda showed them the small laboratory where she blended wines, and the recently refurbished bottling room with its gleaming machinery. They ended up in the tasting room, a section of the main shed that she had set up, decorated and furnished herself as a comfortable place in which to entertain potential clients and friends. It was adorned with colorful posters from wine-growing areas of the world, an old-fashioned winepress, antique bottles, and seats made from barrels.

Gianni had already laid out on the polished jarrah counter several bottles of both red and white wines and a row of tasting glasses, together with the tidbits Dot had provided for the occasion. With ritualistic flourishes, Gianni half filled the small tasters and amid much laughter at their own exaggerated language, the girls gave their verdicts. All were especially enthusiastic about Melinda's gold-medal red.

That night they dined at another local winery, which had recently opened a restaurant. By the end of the evening they were all rather maudlin again, but enjoying their orgy of reminiscing enormously. The only trouble was that for Melinda, for the first time, the past had raised ghosts she would have preferred to have kept decently buried.

Next day they left after breakfast. Although there would probably be opportunities during the next couple of weeks to meet again, separately if not all together, before they dispersed to their other lives once more, goodbyes were, as usual, emotional, and the air rang with promises to be at the next reunion.

Melinda waved until the two cars were out of sight. Then, although she had no regrets about being the one to stay in the valley, the usual flat feeling that came with the end of every reunion weighed her down as she went back inside the house. There was work to be done but she was not in the mood. The imminent fate of Jarrahwood hung over her, and there was also the problem of Matthew. She knew she ought to pick up the phone and talk to Kyle straightaway, yet she still shrank from it.

She was heading resolutely for the office to make the call when a screech of tires in the yard halted her, and she retraced her steps to see who the visitor was. It was Kyle.

"You just missed them," she greeted him as he reached the door, assuming he'd come to say goodbye. "They left about twenty minutes ago."

His dark eyes rested on her face. "I came to see you." He looked tense.

"Come in, then. Would you like some tea? Or coffee?"

"Tea would be fine."

In the kitchen he remained standing while she put the kettle on. There was a long, uneasy silence before he said crisply, "I came over to tell you I'm going back to Sydney in a few days." He added hurriedly, as though an explanation was needed, "I've neglected a number of things that are now clamoring for my attention, and Matthew has to go back to school soon."

"What about Heronvale?" Melinda asked. "Have you settled what's to happen to it?" She could not trust herself to meet his eyes and she was wondering how she was going to tell him about Matthew's plea to stay behind. He was never going to agree, she knew, but she had to ask him because she'd promised Matthew.

His answer to her question surprised her. "My mother will remain there for the time being," he said. "Thanks to Rocky Jacovich, I've managed to find someone to take over managing the place for the next six months, anyway. After that I'll look at the situation again."

Melinda wondered if Mrs. Macintosh had dug in her heels or if Kyle had simply changed his mind. Maybe what she'd said to him had influenced his decision, after all.

"That sounds like a good temporary solution," she said. "I'm sure your mother would be very unhappy if she was forced to leave Heronvale too abruptly."

"She left Italy without a qualm—six weeks after meeting my father!"

"She was in love with your father then. Her roots are here now and it's important to old people to stay where they feel secure, especially when they've lost a loved one. All her memories are here. Her roots are all she has now."

He gave her a long, penetrating look and answered gruffly, "Yes, I suppose you're right."

There was never going to be a better opportunity, so Melinda steeled herself to speak to him about Matthew now. She breathed in deeply. "Kyle—I'm glad you came over. I was wanting to talk to you. In fact, I was about to phone when you arrived. It's about Matthew."

His eyes narrowed, the long lashes almost brushing his cheeks. "Matthew? He hasn't been naughty, I hope."

"No, no, of course not." Melinda busied herself with the tea making, keeping her eyes averted. "It's something he's afraid to talk to you about himself, so he asked me to do it. He's very happy here, Kyle. He doesn't want to go back to Sydney."

"He told you that?" A grim tone had crept into his voice.

"Yes. He's made a good friend of Robert and he likes helping around the vineyard. Rocky says he wants to be a vigneron and your mother apparently suggested he might like to take over Heronvale one day." She dared to look up to see how he was taking it so far.

His face was a mask—grim, unyielding. "He wants to stay with his grandmother," Melinda continued, "and go to school with Robert."

Kyle exploded. "That's a preposterous idea!"

"I don't think it is," she said boldly. "I think it would do him a lot of good and free you of responsibility for a while."

"Did my mother put you up to this?" he demanded.

Melinda bit her lip. "No. Matthew did. I don't think she's been consulted yet. But she'd love to have him, Kyle...."

"Perhaps you're suggesting his grandmother could bring him up better than his father?"

Melinda flinched. "Kyle, how much time do you have to give the boy? You admitted yourself—very little. He could come to Sydney for holidays with you, and his mother." She smiled hopefully. "It's what he wants, Kyle, and I think you should try it. He's happy here, but in Sydney he's faced with conflict. He doesn't see much of you and he feels his mother doesn't really want him. He's heard his stepfather saying unkind things about him to her."

Kyle, looking at the floor, swore softly. Melinda could tell that he was stunned by the proposal and instinctively antagonistic to it.

He looked up suddenly. "I wonder why Matthew thought *you* would be able to persuade me."

Melinda shrugged.

"He could have talked to me himself."

"He's scared of you," she said, without thinking.

"That's ridiculous."

"No, it isn't. You're a rather remote and formidable figure to him. That's not necessarily your fault. You've a busy career and you've been through a lot of emotional stress recently. It's hardly surprising you haven't had as much time for him as maybe he needs. He feels rejected, I think, both by you and his mother. You have your hotels, she has Greg and her career, and he has no one. Here he had his grandmother and Rosa, and his friend, Robert. And, I suppose, me. We get along fine. We're not involved. He doesn't have any emotional complications with us. He *exists* for us, Kyle. He feels that he doesn't for anyone else."

"What are you talking about? He exists for me!"

She could see he was hurting, but she had to go on. "He doesn't feel that. He feels guilty, I think, perhaps even responsible for your marriage breakup."

"That's crazy!"

"Not to a young, vulnerable child. He's tossed back and forth between his parents like an object, not really belonging to either. He feels it must be his fault because he doesn't receive the love he instinctively expects. He thinks you both wish he'd never been born." Kyle groaned aloud and she paused, then pleaded, "Let him stay, Kyle. Maybe just for a semester, as a trial period. It can't do any harm."

He paced to the other end of the kitchen, turning abruptly. "I'm not leaving him in the valley."

The chill finality of his tone offered no compromise.

"Just for a trial period, Kyle," she begged.

"No. He's my son and he'll live with me and be brought up by me. I'm not having him estranged from me. He's suffered a good deal over the past couple of years, I know, but in time he'll adjust."

"I don't think he will, Kyle," Melinda said sadly. "You should realize that Matthew may want a different kind of life than the one you envision for him. You'll have to let go one day."

His jaw was set stubbornly. "Maybe. But in the meantime, I shall bring him up. I'm not having him spoiled by a doting grandmother and her house-keeper. He'd become impossible."

Melinda objected squarely. "I don't think so. Rocky would be a steadying influence. Matthew would learn a lot about family living from the Jacoviches. It would be good for him."

"You've got it all worked out, haven't you?" he muttered angrily.

Melinda moistened her lips anxiously. "Kyle, he needs a break...."

He scowled at her and folded his arms across his broad chest. "I'm returning to Sydney at the end of the week, and Matthew will come with me. He's my son. I don't want him alienated from me. Maybe I'm not doing a very good job of being a sole parent, but I'm trying." Abruptly he half turned away from her, his profile rigid with an anguish he was not able to hide.

Melinda wanted to run to him to comfort him as though he were a child like Matthew, but she dared not. Her own feelings were becoming all too painfully clear to her.

Kyle turned back to her, face stiff with pain. "Matthew is all I have now," he murmured. "I couldn't bear to lose him, too."

Melinda clasped her hands tightly behind her back as she leaned against the counter for support. Did he still love Gina? She supposed he must. "Well, I hope it works out for you," she said. "Both of you."

She felt deeply for Matthew, picturing his disappointment, perhaps blaming her for not trying hard enough. She felt guiltily that she had not, but she could think of nothing more to say. Kyle looked at her bleakly for a moment, gulped his tea down and then with a gruff farewell, left her, with thoughts that had no easy resolution still clamoring in her head.

The thought of Kyle going back to Sydney lay like a lead weight on her heart. His return to the valley had shattered her tranquillity and shown her that she possessed depths of emotion she had not imagined in herself. He had made her realize how lonely she was, how incomplete, how the valley and Riversham and her success were not the recipe for total happiness. There was still an ingredient missing. She knew what it was. Love. She had so much to give and no one to give it to.

Chapter Six

Matthew came down to Riversham next day, eyes red rimmed, mouth truculent, and wept in Melinda's arms.

"He says no," he choked. "He won't let me stay. I've got to go back."

"I'm sorry," Melly whispered, feeling she had somehow betrayed the boy. "I tried, Matthew, but it's only natural for a father to want his son to live with him."

"I hate him!" Matthew grated.

She smoothed his dark hair gently. "No, you don't. Not really. He cares very much for you, Matthew. That's why he doesn't want to leave you here with your grandmother. He's very lonely, you know. He needs you. He suffered a lot when he and your mother got divorced. Have you thought that he might still love her and losing her has made him very miserable?"

She sat on the couch and drew him down beside her. Matthew still looked truculent, bottom lip jutting rebelliously, and Melinda wasn't sure if he was listening, let alone that he might understand what she was trying to say to him. She rumpled his hair. "Try and be patient with him, Matthew. I'm sure things will get better in time."

He flopped away from her and drew his knees up, hugging them. "She got married again. One day, he'll do the same. And I'll have a stepmother as well as a stepfather. She won't want me, either, but she'll have to put up with me because of him. Like Greg does." Sullenly he looked at her. "I heard Greg say once, 'Good God, Gina, I only put up with him for your sake.'"

"That wasn't very nice, but I'm sure he didn't mean to be unkind."

Matthew's mouth twisted. "You don't know what it's like. They don't want you. They want kids of their own or none at all. You're just a nuisance, a mistake, sort of. There's a kid at school, and his parents have been divorced for years. He's got two half brothers and a half sister, and he and his real sister spend half their time at one house, half at the other. He says it's awful, because they don't really belong anywhere."

Melinda tried to be positive. "Not all families are like that. He's unlucky. I'm sure it'll work out better for you, Matthew."

"If you married Dad, you'd want to have children of your own," he accused.

"Yes, but I'd still love you," Melinda protested. "Of course I would. And lots of other people are the same. It doesn't necessarily turn out badly."

Matthew snuggled against her. "I wish you would marry Dad! That'd be ace."

Melinda felt an odd kind of pang under her rib cage. She wouldn't mind being Matthew's stepmother, but for that to happen she and Kyle would have to be in love. And that just wasn't going to happen. "Just be patient, and brave, Matthew. Things will work out." She wished she felt as confident as she sounded.

Matthew swallowed hard and gritted his teeth. With a faint grin he said, "Can we go on a picnic before I have to leave?"

"Why, yes, love, if you want. You're not going till the end of the week. Ask Robert."

"No, not Robert," the child said. "Just you and me and Polly, like we did before. You know, when we went to the bush and looked at birds and you told me scary stories about the bushranger who used to use that old hut, and we swung on the tire and you fell in the river."

Melinda laughed. On a sympathetic impulse, she had taken him out to show him around Riversham the day after the funeral of his grandfather. He'd looked so forlorn at the funeral, she'd tried to cheer him up with the invitation. He hadn't seemed all that keen, but he'd come down to Riversham, and gradually he'd thawed and they'd had an amazingly happy time. He'd met Robert that day, too, but despite his friendship with Rocky's son, he evidently wanted to repeat the first picnic exactly as it had been, with just the two of them. Perhaps, Melinda thought, it was because that day he'd been happy for the first time in a long while. Her heart ached for the small, tousled boy before her

who at this moment no doubt believed he wasn't going
to be happy again—ever.

"If you like," she said. "What about tomorrow?"
She couldn't remember whether there was anything
important she had to do next day, but it didn't matter. She was going to take Matthew on a picnic come
hell or high water. "By the forecast, it's going to be
hot enough to swim, so wear your swimsuit this time."

He brightened at once. "Can I bring Rufus?"

"Of course. He loves playing with Polly. They'll
enjoy a swim, too."

"You won't forget the binoculars, will you?" he
reminded her.

"No, and I won't forget slices of Dot's fruitcake and
Rocky's homemade ginger beer that you like so
much."

He looked at her for a moment, then flung himself
into her arms again, clinging as though he never
wanted to let go.

Melinda was determined to make the farewell picnic a happy day for Matthew, but she knew it would
require considerable effort for her to remain cheerful
herself. There was an awful poignancy about it that
brought tears to her eyes every time she thought about
it. She had become very fond of the boy even in so
short a time and knew she would miss him about the
place.

In a way she was glad they were going, because
Kyle's return had thrown her into more emotional
turmoil than she'd ever thought possible. Once they
were gone, her peace of mind would be restored and
she would be able to get on with the job of running

Riversham, the most important thing in her life. The past could be buried and she would never let it come back like the bushranger's ghost to haunt her again.

Matthew arrived an hour before lunch. He was dressed in jeans tucked into gumboots, and a red-and-blue-checked shirt, and he was carrying a backpack. His dark hair was, for the moment, tidily brushed back, and he looked so like Kyle that Melinda caught her breath. It wasn't that he looked like Kyle now, but that he looked more like the young Kyle, the young man who had also worn checked shirts and jeans tucked into gumboots, and who had carried a backpack on their rambles together.

"Rosa sent some goodies," Matthew said, and with that humorous glint in his eyes Melinda had come to know well, mimicked, "You taka the sausage and the bread, Matteo, and you tella Melinda she not to send a single crumb homa afterward. You hear me, Matteo? You can take some *biscotti* as well if you want. I maka the *cioccolata* chip cookies especially for my *bravissimo bambino!*"

"I don't believe you," said Melinda, laughing.

"She did so say it! And she said I've got to have Italian lessons so next time I come she won't have to start teaching me all over again."

Dear Rosa, thought Melinda. She was either doing her best to keep the boy optimistic or indulging in her own wishful thinking. She wondered what Mrs. Macintosh thought about it all.

As though sensing her curiosity, Matthew said, "Nonna asked Daddy if I could stay on for a while, but he got very angry and said no to her, too, and walked out of the room. She looked sad and when I said I'd come back soon, she heaved a big sigh and said everything could be different in six months. What do you think she meant?''

Melinda thought it best not to tell him that Heronvale might be sold in six months since apparently no one else had mentioned it, so she shrugged it off. ''I don't know, darling. Older people sometimes don't like to plan too far ahead.''

Matthew, in the way of children, let it ride. ''Let's get going,'' he said. ''Where's Polly?''

The usually sedate old kelpie was frolicking with Rufus, and both dogs came bounding up when Matthew whistled and called. ''I wish I could have a dog,'' Matthew said wistfully, ''but Daddy says they're too much trouble, with him being away on business so much. Our housekeeper doesn't like dogs, anyway.'' Triggered by his own remark, he launched into a tirade supposedly by the housekeeper in Sydney about the dirty habits of dogs, and kept Melinda amused for five minutes or more. She was glad to see that despite everything he seemed in good spirits, or was at least putting a good face on it.

Melinda replicated the previous picnic day as closely as possible, sensing that it was important to Matthew that it should be so. They walked down through the vines and she told him about her plans for new plantings, which he listened to attentively, his remarks showing that he had been absorbing a lot of viticulture knowledge during his stay. For a nine-year-old, he had a good head on his shoulders, Melinda thought. In a few years he could probably manage Heronvale standing on his head, if Heronvale was still in the family. It would be a great pity if it was not, but as neither Kyle nor his brother and sister had any personal attachment to it, its fate was doubtless already sealed.

At the old bushranger's hut they paused for a cool drink and Matthew begged for stories about the local antihero, who had not been all that successful but who had acquired a certain glamour nonetheless.

After bird-watching for a while, they strolled on down to the river. On the riverbank pathway, Melinda suddenly felt Kyle's presence acutely, not just from years ago but from her encounter with him there a few mornings previously. Matthew was thrilled when they spotted a heron's nest with young in it, and also some ducks nesting. They watched kingfishers diving for small fish, and in the trees along the riverbank the magpies caroled joyously. They stopped for lunch at the sprawling old red gum whose trunk jutted out across the swimming hole and whose branches still supported the old car tire on the end of a rope.

"Did you wear your swimsuit?" Matthew demanded, standing close to the edge.

"Of course I did," said Melinda. "I've no intention of getting dunked fully clothed like last time." Although it felt warm enough to go swimming, she judged that the water was probably rather cold nevertheless. Still, for Matthew's sake she would brave it.

"Let's have a swim before lunch," said Matthew, unzipping his jeans.

Melinda dumped the cooler beside his backpack in the shade of the old tree and stripped off her shorts and top. She shivered a little in her green one-piece bathing suit, but there was no way she would disappoint Matthew today. He was already ahead of her, grabbing the tire and balancing across it on his stomach, kicking himself off from the tree to swing out across the river.

"Watch out for snags!" she yelled as he reached the extent of the swing and dived through.

There was a loud splash, a fountain of spray and then an energetically dog-paddling Matthew was shouting, "Come on, Melly!" Rufus and Polly were already swimming toward him.

Melinda grabbed the tire as it pendulated back and forth and, sitting in it, swung herself out over the water. As she skimmed Matthew's head he yelled something she didn't catch. She went with the tire as far as her weight would take it, and then as it swung more slowly back toward the bank she dropped off, entering the water a few yards from Matthew. The water was cool but not cold, and more invigorating than she'd expected. She chased Matthew to the bank and they began again the ritual of swinging out on the tire and dropping into the water from various poses on it. Matthew applauded loudly when Melinda did a smooth back somersault and a minute later he was eagerly trying it himself.

Melinda was breathless long before Matthew, so she swam back to the bank and clambered out. She was rubbing herself on a towel when she caught sight of a man striding along the riverbank toward her. Kyle. She tensed, expecting he would upbraid her for letting Matthew use the tire as a diving board. But with her there, what possible harm could come to him? Her suit was still too wet to put her clothes back on so, feeling exposed, she wrapped the towel around her. She raked her fingers through her hair, which was plastered about her face in little corkscrews.

"Hello, Kyle." She greeted him cheerfully, but wondered why he had come. She supposed that his mother or Rosa must have told him where they were going since Matthew probably wouldn't have mentioned it himself—not voluntarily.

"I thought Matthew had gone out for the day with Robert," Kyle said, looking at her as though she had deceived him herself.

His remark and his surprise told her that her assumption had been wrong. He must have just decided to take a walk and had discovered them by accident.

"We decided to have a picnic," Melinda said, ignoring the fact that apparently Matthew had deceived him. "And as it was so warm today, a swim." She looked him over. "Didn't you jog this morning?"

"No." His gaze had drifted to the river where Matthew was still splashing about with the two dogs, having a whale of a time. Either he hadn't noticed his father's arrival or he was deliberately not acknowledging it. He'd expect to be reprimanded, no doubt, for saying he was spending the day with Robert when it wasn't true.

Melinda said, "Matthew swims like a fish."

"They teach them at his school." He was staring at his son in a preoccupied way, answering her in flat tones.

"We found a heron's nest—occupied," Melinda said, wondering how to dispel the awkwardness she felt. "And some ducks nesting. Matthew's becoming quite knowledgeable about birds. He gave me a few tips on planting vines, too!"

Kyle turned to her. "He's been having quite an education these past weeks—Italian from Rosa, viticulture from Rocky and nature study from you."

Melinda heard a touch of sarcasm, but Kyle smiled to belie it and she gave him the benefit of the doubt. "It all makes a change, I suppose," she said.

A shout from the water made her turn back to Matthew. "Come on, Melly!" he was yelling. "Your turn!" He still seemed to be deliberately ignoring his father.

Melinda shouted back, "In a minute." She glanced at Kyle. "What about a swim?" It occurred to her that swimming might have been his reason for coming down to the river. "Was that what you had in mind?"

"As a matter of fact, yes."

"Well, come on in, then." She took a couple of steps down the grassy bank toward the tree and the tire, beckoning.

"No togs," he said.

Melinda stopped. "Oh, I see—you weren't expecting company." A sudden image of Kyle diving nude into the river brought a faint flush to her face, which annoyed her, so she said, "You're wearing briefs, aren't you? I daresay your swim trunks are no more modest."

Kyle hesitated, and Melinda guessed he was wary of causing a scene. Matthew was not very well disposed toward his father at the moment and likely to be resentful of his intrusion on what was meant to be a private outing with Melinda. But it also occurred to Melinda that Kyle's joining in might have some benefits.

"Come on," she urged. "A bit of juvenile horse-play won't do you any harm." What she wanted to say was that Kyle ought to play with his son more.

He still hesitated and for a moment she thought he was going to demur and continue on his way, but all at once he seemed to make a decision and began to unbuckle his belt. Melinda sat in the tire and swung herself out over the water. Matthew tried to grab her legs and pull her down but she avoided him. As she swung back to the tree, Kyle reached it and Melinda's senses reeled a little.

It was ten years since she'd seen him in a swimsuit. There was a little more flesh on his bones now, but it was mainly muscle. His waist was still narrow and hips slim, and the mat of dark chest hair arrowing to the top of his skimpy, dark blue briefs seemed thicker. His olive skin always looked evenly tanned. Unable to prevent it, Melinda cannoned straight into him, and the impact made her shoot out of the tire into his arms. The contact of her skin on his was electric and she stumbled away quickly.

"Go on, your turn," she urged as the tire swung back to them again.

Kyle grasped the tire with both hands and pushed himself halfway through it. Melinda gave him a tremendous push and sent him out over the water, noticing that Matthew was watching in amazement and some apprehension. "Come on, Kyle," she urged silently. "Have fun!"

For an anxious moment she wondered how Matthew would behave. As Kyle swung over the boy's head, Matthew ducked under the water. When Kyle dived in, his son was swimming away from him. Kyle caught up with the boy, shouting something Melinda could not catch, and then the two of them were racing back to the tree.

For the next half hour they dived and swam and indulged in a good deal of horseplay. Melinda was astonished at how relaxed Kyle had become, and watched delightedly when he began to show Matthew some of the tricks he'd performed on a tire when he was a boy. To her relief, Matthew did not seem to resent his father's intrusion, and when they eventually came out of the water to her call that it was time for lunch, Matthew was perched on his father's shoulders. That, thought Melinda, was real progress.

Kyle swung the boy down to the ground. "Mate, you're getting to be a heavyweight!"

Matthew said casually, "Can Dad stay for lunch, Melly? Is there enough food?"

"With what Rosa sent, heaps," said Melinda, spreading the food on a blanket in the shade of a tree. She flung her towel at Kyle. "Do you want to rub down?"

Their eyes met as he caught it, and his drifted down over her, making her realize that bending forward in her swimsuit was somewhat revealing. She tossed Matthew his towel and then casually donned her shirt.

Matthew was less exuberant now and kept casting wary glances at his father, but now and then the two of them chatted in an almost normal way. Melinda did her best to keep up a flow of conversation so there were no awkward moments. Listening to Kyle telling Matthew about the wild things he'd done in Heron Valley as a boy, she was forced into memories of her own, ones she didn't particularly want to resurrect.

But Matthew's wide-eyed interest as he discovered new things about his father was compensation enough. Being a child, he accepted things at face value. If only the fragile rapport that was being established before her eyes could endure, she thought.

With the restlessness of the young, Matthew eventually tired of sitting around talking and listening, and began to throw sticks for the two dogs and to romp with them along the riverbank.

Kyle stretched out lazily, hands behind his head, and said, "I guess I have neglected Matthew. I don't mean to, but pressures..."

"Business pressures are not as important as people," Melinda said. "And sons can be a lot of fun. They grow up all too soon."

"You're right, of course." He turned his head to smile at her. "You've been giving me a hell of a lot of advice lately."

"I'm sorry. I ought to mind my own business."

"Which is Riversham," he said slowly, and narrowed his gaze a little. "Riversham is as much your life as my hotels are mine, especially now you've got the added incentive of a gold medal." He paused, then asked, "Don't you want sons to carry on after you?"

Melinda forced a laugh. "I wouldn't marry for that reason."

Kyle stared at the sky through the leaves. "Friends have told me I ought to marry again because Matthew needs a mother, but I'm not so sure. What if a situation developed like that with Gina and Greg?"

"I guess you'd have to choose who you marry very carefully," Melinda suggested.

"I think I'd rather not risk it," Kyle said, with some bitterness showing. "I'm not exactly enamored of marriage."

"You'll get over that. While you're still in love with Gina—"

He sat up and glowered at her. "I am not still in love with Gina!" His eyes flashed with anger. "I'm not sure that I ever was. She just—happened to me. Gina was a mistake. How we endured each other for as long as we did is a mystery, except that Gina is always reluctant to lose face, and perhaps so am I."

"Matthew was a mistake, too, was he?"

Intense pain replaced anger. "Yes. But, Melly, I don't resent him because of that. It hurts, yes, being reminded of my stupidity, but I don't resent him, and I'm certainly never going to marry anyone who might do so—" He broke off. "What am I talking to you like this for? You can't solve my problems, or Matthew's." A smile broke briefly. "You've got enough of your own with meeting your orders and winning more medals and saving your precious Jarrahwood. What are you going to do about that?"

Melinda was half sorry, half relieved he had changed the subject. She wished she could help him, but his problems were ones that no outsider could resolve. "I'm going to consult some of the environmental groups as soon as I can. There must be someone who's willing to finance it." It was a pity Kyle wasn't, she thought, because he could no doubt afford to. She wouldn't even waste her time asking him.

Kyle rolled over until he was closer to her. He ran his fingertips lightly along her thigh, and smiled at her.

"The trouble is, Melly, whenever I'm around you I still want to make love to you."

She sat up and hugged her knees, resting her chin on them. "Well, after this week that won't be a problem."

He reached up and before she could move out of range, lightly kissed her mouth. He felt the shiver that ran through her and her involuntary response fired him instantly. He held her fast and they rolled over together as he claimed her mouth with urgent need.

Melinda, relaxed and unwary, allowed herself to be submerged in the torrent of feeling that Kyle's warm, hard body aroused, but not quite to drown. She said raggedly, "Kyle—Matthew will see us!"

They rolled apart and looked for the boy but he was nowhere to be seen. The two dogs were sprawled on the riverbank, and the water was like glass again, the tire hanging motionless in the windless air.

The smooth, unruffled water suddenly seemed ominous to Melinda. "Matthew!" she called in a shrill, fearful voice. Oh, God, what if he had gone swimming and got into difficulties and they hadn't even noticed. . . .

"Don't panic!" Kyle's hand clamped her shoulder. "He's around somewhere." He called loudly, "Matthew!"

His voice died away and there was silence. Melinda looked at him in real fear. "Where is he?"

"He probably just got bored and wandered off," Kyle said, but there was a note of real anxiety creeping into his voice.

"The dogs would have gone with him," Melinda said.

They walked down to the edge of the water and the two dogs looked up and wagged their tails.

"Where's Matthew, Rufus?" Melinda demanded.

"They would have made a fuss if—" Kyle said, breaking off as though he did not want to contemplate the possibilities. Melinda knew he didn't necessarily believe what he'd said and nor did she.

For a moment they continued to stare at the still water, innocently dappled by sunlight filtering through the leaves, so stunned they didn't know what to do.

"Matthew!" Kyle's voice was louder, more urgent, vibrating with his own fear.

"Matthew!" Melinda's smaller voice echoed him as she began to run along the riverbank in the direction of the flow. If he'd fallen in somewhere else... The river was full of snags....

Kyle followed, his face contorted now with anxiety. They peered into the debris left by floodwaters, the tangles of roots growing out from the bank, fear growing with every second. Then suddenly from behind them came a shout.

"Hey! Where are you two going?"

Melinda felt the ground shift under her feet as she turned and saw Matthew running along the path toward them, the binoculars bouncing around his neck. The flood of relief was so overwhelming she felt dizzy. "Matthew..." she breathed. "Thank God!"

She felt Kyle's hand grasp hers tightly and, looking up at him, saw him swallow hard. She felt his relief communicated in the hardness of his fingers twined with hers. For long, agonizing moments they had been united in one common emotion—fear—and now in another—relief. Melinda forced back her tears.

"Where have you been?" Kyle demanded of his son, his anxiety translated into anger.

Matthew looked abashed. "I was stalking a bird—back that way." He jerked his thumb over his shoulder in the opposite direction to where they were searching for him. "I heard you calling and came as quick as I could." He looked from one to the other, puzzled. "What's the matter?"

Feeling utterly foolish now, Melinda broke into laughter that verged on hysteria and clasped him to her roughly. "Oh, Matthew. For a minute we thought..." Her eyes met Kyle's. She had learned in those moments of shared panic just how much his son meant to him, and how much the child meant to her. Maybe in those few frantic moments he had learned it, too.

Kyle's anger faded and he laughed, too, roughly tumbling the boy's hair. "For a minute we thought you'd fallen in and drowned. When we saw Rufus and Polly still on the bank..."

Matthew pulled back, his own features relaxing now he realized they were not angry, after all. "I told them to stay so they wouldn't disturb the bird. It was a scarlet robin, Melly, really beautiful." He looked at his father. "How could I drown? I can swim as well as you!"

"You bet you can," said Kyle. "Come on, let's get on with the picnic." He grasped Matthew's hand and the boy slid his other hand into Melinda's. They walked back to the swimming hole. Just as if we were a real family, Melinda thought suddenly.

The thought taunted her for the rest of the day. Kyle stayed until it was time to go back, and it was easy to fantasize that they were a family. Walking beside him, with Matthew carried high on his shoulders again, Melinda let the fantasy weave its spell, and let herself indulge in make-believe for the little time left.

Chapter Seven

Melinda had never found time passing slowly before, but when Kyle and Matthew had gone the days seemed interminable. It wasn't just that spring was merging into summer and the hours of daylight were longer, it was more that she was restless and could never settle down to concentrate on what she was doing to the exclusion of everything else as she had always been able to do before. Kyle and Matthew were constantly in her mind. Were they getting along better or not?

Matthew's unhappiness worried her greatly, but there was nothing she could do about it. There was nothing she could do, either, about the ache deep inside herself that thinking about Kyle brought on. In spite of herself, she had allowed him to intrude on her thoughts and emotions far too strongly. Sometimes her thoughts were so vivid she almost felt he was there, and she would turn joyfully, half believing he'd returned unexpectedly and had crept up on her. But her involuntary and foolish impulse was always in vain. There was never anything but the empty air.

And what if he did come back? What difference would that make? she chided herself. She and Kyle had no future together. When he'd said "Come back with me," he hadn't really meant it. He had his career, and her future lay in running Riversham, improving her wines, winning medals, building a solid customer base for her produce. They were the things to concentrate on. The sparks that still flew between her and Kyle, the strong attraction they still had for each other, were not love.

When an invitation to go to Sydney to a conference of prestigious wine makers arrived, Melinda was astonished and flattered, but for days she wavered about accepting it.

"They'll all be so experienced and knowledgeable," she said to Gianni. "I'll feel such an ignorant fool."

"Nonsense! There will be others like you. You are a gold medal winner, Melly. They will look up to *you*."

"That's kind, but not true. I'll be a very small frog in a very large pond. I'll be out of my depth."

With a very straight face, Gianni answered, "Frogs can swim, even little ones!" He grasped her arms firmly. "Go. You will learn a lot. You want to put Riversham wines on the map, don't you? You need to mix with these other people, learn about marketing and other things. Just making wine is no good, you have to sell it if you want to make a living.''

Melinda acknowledged the sense of what he was saying. For her father's sake, she wanted to achieve for Riversham all that he had hoped for and would have achieved had he lived longer. She owed it to Rocky, too, and her other workers, to build on her success.

Rocky was as forthright as Gianni. ''Of course you must go, Melly. It will open your eyes to a lot of things, give you contacts, boost your confidence. You need to meet people with the same interests as yourself. Besides, you need a holiday. And Sydney's a great place for a holiday.'' He added casually, ''Matthew will love to see you.''

''All right, all right, you've convinced me.'' Melinda laughed. ''I'll go.'' She didn't comment on the possibility of seeing Matthew. She wanted to see him, of course—but did she want to see Kyle?

It was with some trepidation that Melinda prepared for her trip to Sydney. She began to wish she had not been such a stick-at-home, never venturing out of the state. The trouble was, Perth still seemed a long way from anywhere else, even in Australia, despite the fact that you could hop on a plane and be on the other side of the continent in a few hours. The brief holidays she had taken over the years had always been to local places. She had never felt any great inclination to go farther afield. She had never envied her friends their globe-trotting or their glamorous careers.

However, there was excitement, too, in the prospect. ''I feel as though I'm a very late developer!'' she joked rather wryly to Katherine, whom she telephoned to let her know she was coming.

"Better late than never!"

Katherine invited her to stay, and Melinda was grateful. Staying with her would be so much nicer than in a hotel, and she looked forward to seeing Katherine again.

Before she left, Melinda went into Heronbush and bought a couple of new outfits. She chose a smart denim skirt and jacket, a black gabardine skirt and a couple of colorfully patterned silk shirts. Although tempted by a cream-colored linen suit, she decided there was a big enough dent in her bank balance and the dress she'd bought for the Manetti wedding would have to do service yet again for the evening function mentioned on the program. If she went to it, that is. Already she was planning to skip the function because she was bound to feel awkward and shy, not knowing anyone. She would rather take Katherine out to dinner instead. About whether she would contact Kyle or not, she was still undecided. She wanted to see Matthew, but seeing Kyle, too, might provoke emotional conflict again.

She had eased the car into the garage on her return from the shopping trip to Heronbush and was collecting her parcels from the back seat when Rocky appeared, looking rather grim. Melinda's first thought was that something had come up and he would not be able to drive her to the airport tomorrow, after all. Maybe there was a crisis and she wouldn't be able to go. She felt guilty for even thinking that.

"Melly..."

His tone as well as his expression alarmed her. "What's wrong?" Instantly she thought something must have happened to Debra or one of the children. "Rocky, what's the matter?"

He relieved her of the parcels and carried them toward the house, saying, "It's Matthew."

"Matthew!" Her heart constricted. She knew Robert and Kyle's son had been corresponding. "What's happened to him?"

His answer was the last thing she had expected. "He's at our place."

Melinda froze in shock. "At your place? But how...? Why...?"

Rocky carried her shopping inside and dumped it on the kitchen counter. He raked a hand through his hair. "The little blighter came by bus."

Melinda was bewildered. "I don't get this. You surely don't mean all the way from Sydney?"

Rocky nodded. "That's what he says, and he's got the ticket stub to prove it. I don't know how he got away with it, but he reckons everyone believed him when he said he always travels alone by bus to visit his grandmother. He had a whale of a time, I gather, being fussed over and fed by drivers and passengers. He had to change buses in Adelaide, but even that seems to have been no problem."

"Kyle must be frantic," Melinda said. "He'll have been missing for two days or more. He'd never dream Matthew would come here."

"Matthew says he won't be missed because Kyle's in Los Angeles for a conference until the end of the week. Matt's supposed to be staying with his mother, but apparently she rang up and said it wasn't convenient after all and could other arrangements be made while Kyle was away. Matthew took the call, so he kept quiet and when Kyle sent him off to her in a taxi, he made his own arrangements. He managed to stay a couple of nights with one of his school friends without arousing any suspicions and this boy helped him find out about catching a bus to Perth. Under the circumstances, there isn't likely to be a hue and cry for at least a few more days. Not until Kyle returns."

"He'll be missed at school, won't he?"

"Apparently not. Because he was going to be with his mother on the other side of Sydney, he had this week off."

Melinda was shaken. "I've never heard anything like it," she said, and then laughed. "You've got to hand it to him. He's got guts." Her expression sobered. "He must have been very unhappy to run away, Rocky."

He nodded. "Actually, he came here first, and when he found you were out he came down to us. He got a taxi from Heronbush. He had it all worked out and the plan went without a hitch. Not bad for a nine-year-old. I told you he was mature for his age."

"What are we going to do?" Melinda said anxiously. "I suppose we'd better tell Mrs. Macintosh." She paused, then said bleakly, "Kyle will be livid. He just doesn't understand how Matthew feels. If only he'd let the boy stay here awhile."

Rocky nodded. "I reckon that would have been best. Maybe he'll change his mind now."

Melinda wasn't confident. "I doubt it. He loves the boy, Rocky, but he hasn't learned how to form a good relationship with him." It saddened her that the rapport she had seen developing between father and son that day they had picnicked by the river had not lasted. She tightened her lips, saying, "I suppose I ought to take him back with me tomorrow." She appealed to Rocky for advice.

Rocky said nothing, but his expression showed he disagreed with the idea.

"What do you suggest?" Melinda asked. "You've more experience of small boys than I have."

"I think he ought to stay at least until you've had another talk with Kyle."

"But he was adamant he wouldn't allow Matthew to live at Heronvale, not even for a trial period."

"He might have to change his mind. Matthew has discovered that it's fairly easy to run away. Obviously he had access to sufficient money to carry out his plan, but if we send him back he might not come here the next time."

"You're right, of course."

"There are a lot of kids on the streets who've left home," said Rocky. "Some of them no older than Matthew. He could get into a whole heap of trouble." He paused, then suggested, "Let him stay with us for the time being. Maybe you shouldn't even worry Mrs. Macintosh at the moment. Not until you've had a chance to talk to Kyle. You're staying on for a few days after the conference, aren't you?"

"Yes. Katherine insists, and I suppose I ought to see the sights while I'm there."

"You can see Kyle, too."

Melinda quailed inside. Kyle was going to accuse her of interfering again. But for Matthew's sake, she had to try.

"I'd better come home with you and have a chat with Matthew," she said.

"Come to tea," Rocky offered.

Matthew was very subdued when Melinda arrived at the Jacovich house that evening, but when he realized that she was not angry with him he relaxed and after dinner talked freely to her. It seemed that his mother's sudden inability to have him while his father was away had been the last straw. He'd felt totally abandoned and unwanted.

"She didn't want me, anyway," he said morosely. "And Greg hates me. I'm just a pain in the neck. Dad's always out or away. The baby-sitters he gets are the pits. It's hopeless. This kid at school ran away once, so I thought I might as well give it a try."

"You could have got into all kinds of trouble," Melinda pointed out with only as much disapproval as she thought was necessary.

"Not really. I didn't run away to live on the streets like this kid at school did. He got picked up by the police and sent home. I just caught a bus to Perth. I told everyone I was going to stay with my grandmother while my parents were overseas." He chuckled. "Well, it was half true. One of them is."

Melinda shook her head, still amazed. "Why didn't you go to Heronvale?"

"I was going to, but I was afraid Nonna might be angry, so I went to Riversham first, and when you weren't in I came down here." He grinned suddenly. "At first, Mrs. Jacovich thought I'd just come back with Dad for a visit, but when Robert came home from school, he guessed."

"Well, I don't know what we're going to do with you," Melinda said.

"I won't go back!" Matthew cried vehemently.

"And we won't make you," Melinda soothed. "Not right now, anyway. It's a bit of luck I'm going to Sydney tomorrow. I'll talk to your father again, but I can't promise anything."

"I'm not going back, ever," Matthew said truculently.

Melinda could only say, "Well, let's hope we can work something out."

He looked at her intently for a moment. "Nonna told Dad one day that he ought to marry you and come back to Heronvale to live. She said he used to be in love with you when you were younger."

Melinda laughed. "And I suppose he told her that people fall in and out of love quite often when they're young."

Matthew looked amazed. "Yeah, that's what he did say!"

Melinda sighed. "Your grandmother doesn't want Heronvale to be sold, Matt, so I'm afraid she was indulging in a bit of wishful thinking, that's all."

"Well, I wish he'd marry you, too," Matthew said earnestly. "That'd be ace. You could come and live at Heronvale with us, and Rocky could have your house and you could put the new cellarhand Rocky says you're getting in his house."

Melinda rumpled his hair. "If only we could change things to the way we want them!"

"Would you marry Dad if he asked you?" Matthew asked slyly, and Melinda felt a faint blush creeping into her cheeks, surprising herself.

"He isn't likely to ask me," she said, and went on quickly to stop him from probing. "Matt, for a while you might have to do what your father wants. Until you're old enough to decide your future for yourself. You'll have to accept, too, that living at Heronvale and running a vineyard is not what he ever wanted to do. He isn't going to change."

"He used to work on the vineyard before he went away," Matthew said.

"Yes, but it wasn't what he wanted to do most. All the time he was itching to get away."

Matthew looked disconsolate. Grown-ups were a mystery to him. It often seemed to him that his father did not enjoy the work he did now, either. Especially lately. Since they'd returned from the visit to Heronvale, he'd been moody and snappish and given to staring into space and not listening to the things Matthew said to him. It wasn't just because he was annoyed with Matthew for wanting to stay in Western Australia. Matthew sensed that there were other reasons for his father's moodiness.

He wished his father would marry Melly. Melly wasn't like the other women Kyle took out from time to time. She noticed him and talked to him. He always had the feeling that his father's girlfriends, and even his own mother, looked down at him from a great height, even if they weren't actually all that tall. Melly wasn't tall, yet although she was taller than he was, she always seemed to be on his level. He couldn't imagine going on picnics with his father's other women friends. Not the sort of picnics you had with Melly. She was a real sport.

"I wish I was grown up," Matthew complained. "Then I could do what I like and not bother anyone." He brightened briefly. "I can leave school when I'm sixteen. I can come back and learn to make wine. And if Heronvale's been sold, would you give me a job? I'll buy my own vineyard one day, of course."

Overcome by tears and laughter, Melinda impulsively hugged him. "Of course I'd give you a job, darling. I bet you'll make one of the best wine makers this country has ever had. But that's a long way off and you might change your mind in the next few years. There are a lot of exciting things to do in the world and the first one we choose isn't always the right one."

Next morning, sitting in the aircraft, staring out at the amazing cloud mountains in a deep blue sky, Melinda's mind was still partially preoccupied with her conversation with Matthew the previous night. It had been so sharply on her mind she'd had little time for travel nerves that morning. If she was nervous at all it was about her interview with Kyle. Their meeting was still several days away, but she was afraid she would find it difficult to concentrate on her conference in the meantime.

Poor Matthew, she thought as the plane droned on toward Sydney. Poor Kyle.

The flight was over much more quickly than Melinda had expected. Her preoccupation throughout it had made the time pass swiftly. Not that her pondering had been in the least productive, she thought as she gathered her hand luggage and prepared to disembark.

Katherine was waiting for her as promised. Melinda was thankful that there was a familiar face amid all the strangers in this strange city.

"Good flight?" Katherine asked, guiding Melinda to the luggage area.

"Very smooth." Melinda looked around, bemused. "I can't believe I'm actually in Sydney at last. It seems so crazy now that I never came before."

"You'd probably be surprised how many people have never been interstate, let alone overseas," Katherine said. She gestured to the empty conveyor belt. "Your luggage will appear shortly. As soon as we've collected it, we'll go straight home. You'll probably feel like a rest. I'm afraid I've got appointments this afternoon so I'll have to leave you to your own devices for a few hours."

"I hope I'm not putting you out too much."

"Not a bit. It's lovely to be able to return the compliment after the times I've stayed with you. We'll go out somewhere nice for dinner, and you can have an early night and be on top line for your conference tomorrow. When that's over, we'll go sight-seeing. You must see everything while you're here." She added casually, "You'll contact Kyle, I suppose?"

"Yes, I will," Melinda answered. Her anxiety over Matthew and Kyle's likely reaction to her tackling him a second time about the boy staying in the West spilled over. "Actually, Katherine, there's something very important I want to ask your advice about," Melinda said. "It's to do with Kyle . . . and Matthew."

"Medical advice?" queried Katherine, looking very surprised.

"Not really... although perhaps in a way it is. It's a sort of psychiatric problem."

"Now I am intrigued."

"It's a long story. I'll tell you as we're driving."

Melinda's suitcase appeared on the conveyor belt and she pounced on it. At the same moment a voice exclaimed, "Melinda! Katherine!"

She looked around and found Kyle standing a few feet away. Katherine looked as astonished as she was. "Kyle!"

Melinda just stared. She couldn't believe her eyes. "Kyle... I thought you were overseas."

His eyes narrowed a little. "How did you know that?"

Melinda realized she'd made a faux pas. "Matthew told me."

"You've been talking to Matthew?"

Melinda could not wait now for Katherine's advice. She had to tell Kyle right away, but not here in front of passengers waiting for their luggage.

"You weren't supposed to be coming back until the end of the week," she said, flustered at being caught so unprepared.

"I was able to hurry things up a bit," he answered gruffly. "And cut a couple of days off the trip. I stopped over in Brisbane and then took an internal flight." He looked her over meticulously. "What are you doing in Sydney?"

Caught completely unprepared, Melinda was quaking inside. "I—I'm here for a wine-makers' conference—and a few days' holiday. I'm staying with Katherine."

"I see. How did you get on to Matthew? He's staying at his mother's this week. Did he call you? Is he in the habit of doing that?" The questions were rapped out in a staccato manner, full of suspicion.

"No, Kyle, he doesn't call. He just ran away and came—" Melinda broke off at his sharp intake of breath. Even Katherine gasped audibly. "He's at Rocky's place. He's fine," she reassured him quickly.

"He's over *there?*" Kyle sounded incredulous. "In God's name, how did he—"

"Kyle, I'll explain, but not here," Melinda said, glancing around. A new batch of luggage was coming through. "Is this the luggage from your flight?"

He glanced away from her impatiently, saw a briefcase and a soft-pack suitcase and retrieved them, then turned back to the two women.

Kyle's expression was grim. "Why didn't you bring Matthew back with you?"

"Kyle, can we go somewhere less public and talk?" Melinda begged anxiously.

Katherine had a suggestion. "Kyle, I've got appointments this afternoon. Obviously you and Melly need to talk privately about this. If you wouldn't mind taking her home..."

Kyle nodded. "All right. Yes, I'll do that."

Melinda had no option but to agree. "Sorry about this, Katherine."

Katherine was searching in her handbag. "Here's a spare key to the apartment."

She hurried away leaving Melinda feeling like flotsam on a strange shore. The possibility of meeting Kyle at the airport had not even entered her mind, and she was caught completely off guard. She'd expected to have at least two or three days in which to armor herself against him, and to prepare her case for Matthew with Katherine's help. Now she was thrown in at the deep end.

Kyle said brusquely, "Let's go." He handed her his briefcase and picked up both her suitcase and his own.

Melinda followed him to the parking lot. "I've got Katherine's address somewhere," she said, opening her handbag as he started the engine.

"I know where she lives," Kyle answered abruptly.

Melinda shot a swift glance in his direction. Had he been seeing Katherine, dating her since they'd met again? A pang of jealousy assailed her. But she had no right to be jealous, she reminded herself. No right and no reason.

Kyle swung the car out of the airport and headed toward Sydney. "Now, for God's sake, Melly, tell me how and why my son comes to be in Western Australia." He directed a brief glance at her, and his face was taut with anxiety.

Melinda felt a strong compassion for him. It was no joke being a sole parent. As quickly as she could she explained how Matthew had arrived, and how she had found herself in a dilemma over what to do about him.

"I would have phoned you, naturally," she said, "if you'd been at home, but Matthew said you weren't and I believed him. I didn't think there was much point in worrying his mother," she finished dryly.

He let out a deep breath. "You were right about that." He glanced at her and again demanded, "Why didn't you bring him back with you?"

Melinda swallowed and tried to approach the situation dispassionately, but with him so close to her it was hard. "Kyle, we need to discuss this calmly and rationally," she said. "Although he seems pretty cool about it all, Matthew is in a very distraught state and I thought—so did Rocky and Debra—that it was best to let him stay with them for the time being until something could be sorted out. I know it's a very difficult problem but I'm sure we can find a solution."

"We? It's really none of your business, Melly."

Melinda bridled. "When a small, distressed boy turns up on my doorstep, Kyle, it is my business. He's got no one to tell his troubles to, no one who understand how he feels, or even wants to. Can't you imagine how he felt with you going away and his mother too busy to have him to stay with her? He feels he's the last consideration on anyone's agenda."

Dark eyes flashed at her. "If I'd known Gina was going to act up, I wouldn't have gone to the damned conference."

"No, perhaps you wouldn't have, but the fact remains that Matthew is unhappy, Kyle. Surely you can see that. This being batted back and forth like a ball between parents who both seem much too busy to bother much with him is breaking him up. The best thing that has happened to him all year was you taking him to Heron Valley. He made a friend of Robert, the help he gave Rocky was appreciated, he felt he meant something to people. He felt he *belonged,* and he doesn't feel that either with you or with his mother."

"And you also made him feel loved, which neither his mother nor I do." Kyle's tone was bitter and self-accusing.

"I don't know if that's true."

"Oh, it is. He never stops talking about you."

"I'm sorry."

"No, I am. I didn't mean to sound ungrateful. I'm a bit shocked by the whole thing. I should have made sure he actually arrived at Gina's, but he's been so many times before. . . . Hell, Melly, I know the situation here isn't ideal, but I don't want to lose my son. I don't want him to grow away from me. If he stays in the West his grandmother will smother him. I'll be no more than a distant relative."

"Kyle," Melinda said tentatively, "it's what's best for Matthew that counts. I admit I'm not sure I know what that is. But he thinks, at this moment, that being at Heronvale or Riversham is what he wants."

"A nine-year-old doesn't know what he wants!"

"That isn't the point. The more you deny him, the more he's likely to rebel. You'll lose him more easily that way." She paused, wishing his attitude would soften, but understanding his fears. "Kyle, let him give it a trial. If it's just a novelty he'll soon grow out of wanting to stay for good."

She glanced at his profile. His jaw was set and she could tell he was still resisting the proposal. She could see he was suffering, too. She said, "Don't do anything rash, Kyle. Let the situation cool a little." She felt she had not said enough, that she had presented a very poor argument and had let Matthew down again. But bumping into Kyle at the airport had ruined her whole approach. Instead of confronting him with a well-thought-out case, here she was mumbling and stumbling over her words and not sounding in the least convincing. And it didn't help that his sudden appearance had set her own feelings in turmoil.

There was a long silence, then Kyle said, "I must say it was a shock to see you at the airport. I never thought to see you in Sydney. Spreading your wings at last, eh?"

"Gianni and Rocky persuaded me to come. I'm not really looking forward to the conference. I don't know anyone."

"You soon will." The men would flock around her like bees to a flower, he thought, and with a shock realized he was jealous.

As he seemed anxious to head off any further discussion of Matthew, Melinda judged it might be diplomatic not to push too hard at the moment. She didn't reply to his remark, but allowed the silence to deepen as she looked out the window at the unfamiliar streetscape of Sydney. When she caught her first glimpses of the harbor—a distant view of the Harbour Bridge arched against the clear cobalt sky, then the white sails of the Opera House—she exclaimed aloud. Kyle again turned briefly, this time actually to smile at her.

"After the conference you'll have to go sight-seeing. There's a lot to see in Sydney." His softer tone might have been to atone for his earlier grittiness.

"I know. So I'm staying on for a few days. Katherine's promised to show me around."

"I hope it doesn't rain. We've had nothing but deluges for months."

They were off the main highway now, driving along tree-lined streets with large houses set well back from the road in spacious gardens. Kyle swung the car into the driveway of one of them. Melinda glanced at him, puzzled.

"I thought Katherine lived in a high rise."

"She does. This is my place."

"But I thought we were going to her apartment."

"I changed my mind," he said, scrunching to a halt on the gravel and switching off the engine. His dark eyes rested pensively on her face, and one hand lightly tapped the steering wheel. With false heartiness he said, "I thought you might care to see where I live."

Melinda got out and looked around her. "It looks very grand." The house was red brick, two story and probably Edwardian. That surprised her a little, since she'd imagined Kyle in an ultramodern residence. The grounds were extensive and very secluded.

Kyle led her to the front entrance. She followed him through a spacious hallway into a large room that seemed to extend the full width of the rear of the house. In real estate advertisements it would be called an "entertainment area," she thought wryly. Facing her was a wall of windows and through them she encountered a view of the harbor that was so breathtaking, Melinda exclaimed, "Kyle—this is fantastic!"

Kyle strolled to her side. "Yes, isn't it?"

Melinda was entranced. "What a superb situation." She crossed to the windows. Outside was a wide terrace, and beyond it a sloping lawn, with another terrace below and a swimming pool.

"Sit down," Kyle invited. "Tea or coffee or something stronger?"

"Tea, please," Melinda said. She sank into one of the large, comfortable cane armchairs, mesmerized by the panoramic view through the windows.

Kyle returned in a few minutes with a tray and set it on a table near her.

"There's nothing much to eat," he apologized. "I didn't bother to let my housekeeper know I was coming home earlier." He straightened up. "I'm sorry—I suppose you'd like to freshen up?" She looked perfectly fresh, he thought, finding it difficult to take his eyes off her. She was quite captivating in her smart silk shirt and pencil-slim skirt and her high heels.

Melinda nodded. "Yes, please."

He showed her to a bathroom and when she returned he was sprawled in one of the chairs, hands clasped across his chest, staring through the windows. Melinda caught a strange expression fleetingly cross his face. "I never expected to entertain a Heron Valley gold medalist in my house," he marveled, but his light tone sounded forced.

"I never expected to be here." Melinda avoided looking directly at him. She was ill prepared and not sure how to cope.

He poured a cup of tea for her and she sipped it slowly, concentrating on the fine bone china and wishing she wasn't alone with Kyle, yet perversely not wanting to be anywhere else. He asked her about the conference she had come to Sydney to attend. It didn't take long to tell him, and the conversation seemed to founder afterward. Melinda wanted to talk about Matthew again, but was afraid to, so she asked Kyle how long he'd lived in the house.

"Three years. It was very run-down. Gina fell for the view—the house just happened to go with it."

"It looked quite large from the front," Melinda remarked.

"Too big for Matthew and me," he agreed. "We rattle around in it like a couple of peas in a jar. I spent a fortune restoring it so Gina would have somewhere palatial to entertain her friends.'' His eyes clouded and narrowed. ''Gina was so enthusiastic at first. Things weren't going well for us, hadn't been for a long time, and I thought it might improve matters, but it didn't.'' He linked his fingers and stared at the floor. ''Whatever I did for Gina, it was never enough.''

How he must hurt, Melinda thought, almost regretting taking Matthew's part. Could she blame Kyle for wanting to keep the boy with him?

''I suppose you're tired,'' Kyle said. ''I'd better take you home to Katherine's.''

''I am a bit,'' Melinda admitted. But it was emotional, not physical, weariness she felt. The strain of being with Kyle, of not knowing what to say or how to say it, was telling on her. She felt she had to say something more before she left. ''Kyle, you will think about it, won't you?'' she said, getting up. ''About Matthew.''

He rose, too. ''I've never stopped thinking about it since I left Heronvale.'' And, damn it, he thought, you've been on my mind nearly as much!

He led the way to the door and Melinda followed, incapable of denying any longer, now that she had seen him again, what she had tried so hard to deny for all these past weeks—the simple, agonizing truth that she still loved Kyle.

Chapter Eight

"Do you think there's any chance now that Kyle will give in and let the boy stay at Heronvale, at least for a while?" Katherine asked.

They were having dinner at a small Italian restaurant just around the corner from Katherine's apartment block. Melinda had told her the whole story about Matthew's escapade, and what Kyle had said.

"I don't know. Matthew's so unhappy with the way things are, but naturally Kyle doesn't want to part with him. I hope he takes time to think about it and doesn't just phone up and insist that Rocky put him on the next plane to Sydney."

Katherine nodded. "Poor little kid. He has no proper roots. He's the kind of person who needs a solid base, a safe haven, a place he feels he belongs to." She smiled. "Like you."

"But he wasn't born in the valley, as I was."

"That doesn't matter. People sometimes put the deepest roots down in an adopted environment. Many migrants do. Look at Kyle's mother, for instance." She regarded Melinda closely. "It's a pity Kyle doesn't take after her—then he'd be willing to run Heronvale, and that would solve quite a few problems."

"If he'd been so inclined, Matthew wouldn't have existed."

Katherine laughed. "No, he'd have married you and produced somewhat different little Macintoshes."

"Not necessarily me," Melinda said. "Our romance probably wouldn't have lasted, but I suppose he might have married a valley girl."

Katherine inclined her head. "Why do you think it wouldn't have lasted?"

Melinda shrugged. "Instinct, I suppose. We were young and passion isn't the same as love." That she had discovered that in her case it was, she did not add, but asked, "You've seen Kyle's house?"

"Yes. Beautiful place, but far too large for a two-person family, never mind a man alone."

"And Kyle's definitely not a loner. I can't see him staying single for long. It can't be much fun being a sole parent."

"I don't think he'd marry just to provide Matthew with a stepmother," Katherine said. "He'll be wary of repeating his mistake with Gina. Reading between the lines, I'd say he was more than a little relieved to see her go. It was not a happy marriage."

"He's talked to you about it?" Melinda wondered how close a relationship had developed between Kyle and Katherine since the reunion at Riversham. Katherine hadn't said much about it so far. Thinking of them together gave Melinda such pangs of jealousy that she felt ashamed. She had no right to resent Kyle and Katherine getting together. Quite apart from any physical attraction there might be, they had in common the fact that both had been divorced. Katherine would be able to empathize with Kyle about that. And Katherine would make a good mother for Matthew. She was much more Kyle's kind of person, too.

Katherine answered Melinda's question cautiously. ''A little,'' was all she would say.

Melinda found the conference both exhausting and stimulating. She had not known what to expect, never having been to any kind of seminar or conference before, and she was full of apprehensions when she arrived at the conference centre in the heart of Sydney on the first day. The thought of being among so many people in the wine business terrified her.

But by the time the first session was over, Melinda's attitude had changed completely. She was fascinated by the papers being delivered and scribbled masses of notes. At coffee break and lunch she amazed herself by actually talking to strangers about Riversham and her wines with enthusiasm, and discussing wine making with more confidence than she'd ever felt possible.

She told Katherine, ''I've had a fantastic day!''

Katherine laughed. ''Well, I'm glad it was worthwhile going.'' She paused, wrinkled her nose and then sneezed loudly. ''Oh, dear, I'm afraid I'm getting a cold.''

That Katherine's cold might change the whole complexion of her stay in Sydney did not at that moment occur to Melinda.

The second and final day of the conference was as enjoyable as the first, and by the evening Melinda was no longer hesitant about attending the function, a dinner dance and wine tasting. It was well after midnight when a taxi delivered her back to Katherine's apartment block.

Next morning she was awakened by the telephone ringing. A few moments later Katherine came in.

"Melinda?"

"Yes..." Melinda yawned and flung the bedclothes back. "Oh, look at the time!" It was after ten. She was surprised to see Katherine was still in her dressing gown, and a second glance revealed that she was not looking at all well. "Katherine, you look ill!"

Katherine smiled wanly. "I hate to admit it, Melinda, but I've got the flu." She supported herself against the doorpost. "I'm afraid I won't be able to take you sight-seeing today. I'm so sorry."

Melinda leaped up. "You're not to worry about that. You must go straight back to bed." She threw on her dressing gown. "What can I get for you? Have you had any breakfast? Can I go down to the pharmacy for anything?"

Katherine greeted her concern with a smile. "Thanks, but I've had some tea and toast and that's all I feel like. I just need to sleep it off. It's probably one of those twenty-four-hour viruses and I'll be right as rain tomorrow. Now, listen, that was Kyle on the phone. I told him I wasn't able to drive you around today, so he offered to, instead."

"Oh, no!" Melinda was taken aback.

"What's wrong with that?"

Melinda regretted her involuntary exclamation. "Nothing, really...."

Katherine gave her a slightly exasperated look. "You'd better get showered and dressed. He'll be here at eleven."

"But, Katherine," Melinda protested, "I'm not going out, not when you're sick. You'll need lunch and—"

"I'll need nothing of the kind. All I need to shake this off is a good rest. There's no point at all in your tiptoeing about the flat all day. Go out and let Kyle show you the sights. You can't refuse now, anyway. He'll be here shortly."

Melinda was surprised that he had offered to take her sight-seeing. Had Katherine asked him to and he'd felt he couldn't say no? She was just putting on lipstick when the doorbell pealed.

"Good morning." Kyle came in behind a large bunch of roses, which he thrust into her hands. He grinned at her startled look. "Not for you! For the invalid, to cheer her up a bit."

Melinda's gaze slid across his handsome face with a painful twisting of her heart. "It was kind of you to offer to drive me around, but you don't have to. I can easily—"

"Of course you can't!" He gave her a slightly whimsical look. "I have a free day. I'm not officially back in my office until next week. I can take a holiday, too."

"I do appreciate it," Melinda said meekly, dragging her eyes from his. "I'll just put these in water. Won't be long."

When Melinda carried the vase into Katherine's bedroom, Kyle was perched on the end of the bed, chatting to her. Melinda could not help wondering again if their relationship had been, or even still was, intimate. The thought cast a shadow.

"My favorite yellow roses," Katherine said, smiling affectionately at Kyle. "Thank you. Just what I needed to brighten my day. Now you two go and have a great time and don't worry about me. I'll be fine. I'm just going to sleep the day away. I've put the answering machine on, so I won't be disturbed by anyone. I'm not expected at the hospital for a couple of days, anyway."

"Are you sure you'll be all right?" Melinda asked doubtfully.

"Perfectly all right. Off you go. I want to go back to sleep. Look after her, Kyle. She's in the mood for anything!"

So much was packed into that day that Melinda felt quite dizzy at the end of it. After lunch at a restaurant with a harbor view, they toured the Opera House and crossed the Harbour Bridge. They bought coffee and buns from a street stall, then caught a ferry to Manly.

"The zoo we'll do another day," said Kyle, pointing out Taronga Park on the harborside hill.

He rested one arm across Melinda's shoulders and she did not shrug it away. It shamed her, but she couldn't help wishing Katherine would still be under the weather tomorrow and the next day.

"I don't think I should take up your time for more than one day," Melinda said to appease her conscience. "You must be busy."

"Let me be the judge of that," he said, smiling down into her eyes and effectively stilling her protest.

"Well, it's very kind of you."

He gave her a sudden squeeze. "Oh, Melly, stop acting so formal! We're old friends, aren't we?"

She had to say, "Of course."

It was late when they returned from Manly, and as they drove away from the parking spot where Kyle had left his car, he said, "Would you like to go to a party tonight?"

"I thought you weren't telling anyone you were back."

"I wasn't going to, but I was invited before I went away. Jane and Richard are very good friends and were disappointed I couldn't come. So I called and said I could, after all."

"They don't know me."

"There's no need to feel shy. The Ryans are very friendly and easygoing."

He seemed to want her to go with him, so she said, "What do I wear?"

"We go as we are. Casual. As it's been a warm day, I daresay it'll be a barbecue."

"I feel a bit grubby. I'd like to go home and have a shower," Melinda said.

"No problem," Kyle answered.

It wasn't until Melinda became aware that the streetscape was vaguely familiar that she realized where they were going. Not back to Katherine's apartment, but to Kyle's house again. She sat bolt upright. "I thought you were taking me back to Katherine's."

"There's no need to disturb her," said Kyle smoothly. "You can shower at my place just as easily. You don't need to change your clothes. You'll be fine in that gear."

Kyle showed her to a bathroom upstairs and handed her a big, fluffy gold bath towel. "You'll find everything you need in the way of toiletries in the cabinet," he told her. "You can use the bedroom just opposite." With a wave of his hand he indicated a half-open door.

Melinda undressed in the guest bedroom and spread her shirt and slacks out across the bed to smooth out some of the creases. She wrapped the huge bath towel around her and, barefoot, padded across the deep-piled carpet to the bathroom. She checked the cabinet and found that as Kyle had said it contained everything she could possibly need. Even a hair dryer. That persuaded her to shampoo her hair, which felt sticky from the wind and spray off the harbor.

She decided to dry her hair in the bedroom. With the big bath towel wound around her, she opened the bathroom door and was about to cross to the bedroom when Kyle emerged from another room farther along the passageway. Judging by the damp hair curling around his collar and temples, he had already showered. Melinda should have kept on going, but she paused, hair dryer in hand, and said, "Oh, hi," feeling rather foolish.

Kyle stopped beside her, looking down into her face. He lifted a damp lock of her hair. "Washed your hair?"

"Yes, I'm sorry, I must have taken longer than I thought. You're ready."

"No rush." A large, warm hand strayed to her shoulder and moved lightly over her skin, skimming smoothly up the sinew in her neck to clasp her jaw and tilt her chin. She couldn't avoid his eyes and was alarmed to see that they were smoldering now with the desire he wasn't even trying to conceal. His mouth descended on hers with a gentle pressure, and his other hand moved with tantalizing slowness across the swell of her breasts above the tightly tied towel. Melinda recognized that her feelings could easily become uncontrollable, but her lips responded to his instinctively and she could not make them do otherwise.

Kyle suddenly stepped back. "You'd better get dressed before we both forget we're going to a party."

Melinda rushed quickly into the bedroom and closed the door. Her whole body felt flushed and hot. She swiftly dressed in her slacks and shirt, then blow-dried her hair. She tied the scarf she had worn for most of the day around her hair and fashioned it into a floppy bow. The effect, she thought, approving her reflection, was passably attractive.

Kyle drove her home to Katherine's after the barbecue. As usual when driving, he didn't say a great deal and Melinda wasn't disposed to talk, either. She was, she discovered, quite exhausted.

"Lovely evening, Kyle," she murmured sleepily as they emerged from the elevator at Katherine's floor.

"Thanks for taking me. I enjoyed it very much." That was true. His friends had welcomed her and she had found to her surprise that a lot of people were interested in vine growing and wine making.

Kyle looked at her. She had a glow about her that he'd never seen before. "What about tomorrow?" he said at last. "I daresay Katherine still won't feel up to going out."

Melinda couldn't say no. "If you're really sure you can spare the time."

"Positive." Unexpectedly, he brushed his lips across hers as he said, "Good night, Melly."

The next day Katherine was feeling better, but for a few days she was still weak and tired easily. She was delighted that Melinda's sight-seeing had been taken over by Kyle and she told herself she had no intention of becoming fit enough to interrupt their chance of togetherness.

Kyle took Melinda to the zoo, the art gallery and the Botanic Gardens. They explored The Rocks—the old colonial part of Sydney that had been restored—and the newer Darling Harbour complex. They went to the theater to see a play and the Opera House for a concert. Kyle also took her farther afield, to the Blue Mountains for a spectacular trip across the Jameson Valley by cable car, and to Jenolan Caves to marvel at the stalactites and stalagmites. He seemed determined to show her everything there was to see in and around Sydney. At his persuasion, and with Katherine's encouragement, Melinda stayed longer than she had first intended. Katherine eventually went back to work, but Kyle still seemed happy to take Melinda around.

"Don't you have to work?" she asked him more than once.

"I find there's nothing urgent requiring my attention at the moment," he insisted with a smile. "And I am the boss, after all!"

When at last the time came to leave, Melinda's feelings were mixed. One half of her wanted to go home, the other half didn't want the Sydney idyll to end.

Her flight home was on Sunday, and on Saturday morning she went shopping by herself. Katherine was better and they were both invited to Kyle's for a pool party that afternoon. Melinda had not brought a swimsuit and Katherine's were too big for her, so her first purchase was a one-piece maillot in a peachy color that toned beautifully with her hair.

After buying it she spent the rest of the morning strolling around the department stores and exploring the arcades, browsing for presents to take home. As a result, she arrived back at Katherine's apartment later than she'd expected. Katherine was already dressed to go out, but not to Kyle's party.

"I've got to go to the hospital urgently," she said apologetically. "I've let Kyle know and he's coming to pick you up in about an hour. Have you had any lunch?"

"No, I haven't."

"I thought you might not have, so I made an extra sandwich. It's in the fridge."

"Thanks." Melinda was disappointed. "I've hardly seen anything of you, Katherine."

"That was my fault. I'm sorry, Melly. You'll have to come over again some time. But I'm glad Kyle was able to spare the time to take you around. It wouldn't have been much fun on your own. Thank heaven you haven't caught the flu. If you'd mooched around the flat trying to be Florence Nightingale, you probably would have.'' She glanced at her watch. ''I have to go. Have a good time, and don't forget you're catching a plane in the morning!''

Melinda hurriedly ate the sandwich Katherine had left her, then changed into her new swimsuit and slipped shirt and jeans on over it. She stuffed underwear and makeup into her bag and tied a scarf loosely around her hair. She was just ready when Kyle arrived.

''It's a shame about Katherine,'' she said as they went down in the elevator. ''And I feel I've neglected her shamefully. I've been using her place as though it was a hotel.''

''I don't think she minds,'' Kyle said.

Melinda fastened her seat belt. ''Well, I must say it's been a fabulous holiday. Thanks to you, Kyle.''

He smiled at her rather enigmatically. ''You've enjoyed yourself?''

''I've had a ball!''

''But you'll be glad to be going home?''

She glanced at him furtively. His profile gave nothing away. ''Yes, of course,'' she answered. ''I keep worrying about what's happening, and having to stop myself from phoning Rocky to find out.''

''You're a very dedicated lady,'' he said dryly.

Melinda was surprised when they arrived at his house to find that no one else was there yet.

''Where is everyone?'' she asked innocently.

He gave a slightly sheepish grin. "They couldn't come. Funny how busy people are on a Saturday afternoon sometimes."

Melinda realized she'd been duped. "You thought I might not come if I knew we'd be alone? Katherine didn't have an urgent call, did she? She just went out until you'd collected me, in case I twigged. What's the idea, Kyle?"

"There's no need to be so suspicious."

"Why, Kyle?" Melinda persisted uneasily. "Why did you ask me here alone?"

"It's your last day. I thought a nice, relaxing afternoon swimming, and later a light meal, some good music and conversation..." He smiled, inviting her to object. "Anything wrong with that?"

There wasn't, except that she was alone with him at his house, and it was much more intimate here than in any of the places they had been all week. Melinda said doubtfully, "No, I suppose not." Why had he done it? she wondered, not quite believing his glib explanation. A wild hope jerked into her mind, but she hardly dared catch hold of it.

"Let's start with a swim. You brought a bathing suit, I hope."

"I'm wearing it."

Kyle showed her to a pine cabana, half concealed amid the lush semitropical shrubbery that formed a backdrop to the pool on two sides. There she found a shower cubicle and several fluffy gold towels. She peeled off her clothes and then felt reluctant to reveal herself. It was a moment or two before she could bring herself to walk boldly out of the cabana to the poolside. Kyle was not there. On the patio was a large umbrella sheltering two white tubular-steel lounges with colorful mattresses. Melinda paused for a moment on the edge of the glittering water, raised her hands above her head, arched her body and dived in. As the water closed over her head she heard a shout of "Bravo!"

Melinda shivered briefly at the shock of the cool water, but the brisk swim to the other end of the pool warmed her. As she turned, there was another splash and Kyle joined her.

"Race you to the other end," he challenged.

He won, of course, and she swam into his waiting arms, breathless but exhilarated. He held her tightly and kissed her. His lips tasted of chlorine.

"Unfair advantage," Melinda accused, trying to pull away.

Kyle linked his hands around her waist and kept her a prisoner. "Wet or dry, you're still the most enchanting woman I know," he murmured. He raised one hand to touch her hair, which was plastered about her face as his was, and there was laughter as well as desire in his eyes. "Even with your hair all flat!"

And he was the handsomest man she knew, she thought, any way he was.

"I wonder if I can still backstroke," Melinda said as an excuse to get away from him. Taking him by surprise, she ducked under his arm and submerged herself. With a good start on him she reached the other end of the pool first, turned and found herself hurtling slap-bang into his outstretched arms again.

"Let me go!"

Kyle picked her up and then dropped her back into the water. She sank like a stone, to surface seconds later spluttering and shaking the drops off her face, glaring at him with a baleful look. Vengefully she lunged and he was too slow to avoid the return ducking. As he surfaced, she was already clambering out of the pool. Kyle grabbed an ankle and pulled her back in. She collapsed in his arms once more, too breathless to fight anymore, and too weak to resist the kiss that seemed to go on forever as they stood in the shallow end, closely entwined, lost in the sheer pleasure of the intimate contact of their bodies. It had to break at last, but they drew apart slowly, both deeply shaken.

Melinda slid smoothly into the water and with a lazy stroke that barely disturbed the surface, headed for the other end of the pool. She was, she realized, in danger of succumbing to Kyle's carefully planned seduction. For that was all this was. She still had the power to arouse him, but there was no consolation in that when what she needed was the power to make him love her.

Kyle did not swim after her this time, but climbed out, and was toweling himself when she walked slowly back along the pool's edge to the loungers. He threw a towel to her.

Melinda gazed out across the harbor, shimmering blue in the afternoon sun, dotted with yachts, and then let her eyes drift leisurely back to the glossy umbrella trees reflecting the sunlight, the brilliant reds, pinks and yellows of the hibiscus bushes, the flamboyant stalks of the rock orchids and the flaming foliage of crotons and Fijian fire bushes.

"It's a wonderful garden," she remarked. Kyle's gaze made her skin tingle as though he was actually touching her. She dropped her towel over the end of the lounger and stepped back into the sun to finger-comb her hair, her back to him. It was a shock when she felt his fingers tangle with hers.

"Hey..." Her protest faded as he smiled at her. She lowered her hands and let him ruffle her damp locks dry. His gentle massage of her scalp was both relaxing and arousing. She didn't resist when he scooped her up and carried her to one of the loungers, placed her on it and lay beside her. The narrowness of it necessitated his lying very close.

"It's nice to have you here," he murmured.

"It's nice to be here." And I want to be here with you all the time, she thought, and wondered what he would say if she gave voice to the thought.

His lips nuzzled against her ear, he nibbled her lobe and trailed kisses down her neck, making every nerve in her body tense with anticipation. Lightly he peeled back the top of her swimsuit to bring exquisite pleasure to her already hardening nipples and the sensitive skin of her swelling breasts. Sensations rolled through her that were new and irresistible.

"Kyle..." she moaned, thrusting instinctively against him to heighten the pleasure he was already giving her.

He lifted his head and looked at her. Desire clouded his gaze and darkened the already dark pupils. His lips were full and faintly moist and there were fine drops of perspiration on his upper lip. His almost-naked body was warm and possessive on hers and it was becoming so easy to forget everything except the joy of being in Kyle's arms, even easy to persuade herself that it could last forever...if she told him how she felt and that despite what he believed, the valley and Riversham would no longer claim her if he did....

"I think we'd better go inside," Kyle murmured.

The sound of his voice, husky with desire, finally pricked the fragile little bubble of euphoria that had ballooned inside her. She faced reality. She was going home tomorrow. And Kyle had invited her here today because he wanted to make love to her. She had let him see that she was aroused by him, and he'd probably thought she just needed the right surroundings and atmosphere. He hadn't asked her here to tell her he loved her... only that he wanted her. If in the past week, and even more in the past hour, she had allowed a wild hope to be born—that his passion could turn to love—that was her foolishness. She had always loved him, although she had pretended otherwise, but as she'd always known, he had never really been in love with her.

She freed herself from his embrace and, covering herself, stood up. "Kyle, I think I'd better go," she said, moving away jerkily. "Don't bother. I'll get dressed and call a cab."

Her sudden move had taken him by surprise, and for a moment he just stared at her numbly. Now he reacted. "You can't go yet!" He leaped up and grasped her arms, shaking her. "Melly—for God's sake..."

"Please—let me go." She moistened her lips nervously.

He crushed her against him hard. "Don't you feel anything at all for me?"

She nodded, with a pale smile. "It's just chemistry, Kyle," she murmured, "and some nostalgia, I guess." The lie was hard to speak, but she had too much pride to tell him the truth and not enough courage to hear him tell her he was sorry, that although he still found her attractive as a woman, he wasn't in love with her. She loved him so sweetly, yet so bitterly, it was like a deep knife wound.

Silence engulfed them for painful moments, then he said with rough dismissal, "Go and get dressed, and then I'll drive you back to Katherine's."

Chapter Nine

As he carried Melinda's suitcase from the airport terminal to the car, Rocky said, "You look tired, Melly."

"It was hectic," she admitted wearily. Let him think her lack of spirit was physical, not emotional.

"Glad to be back?"

"I can't wait to get home." And yet, for once, the prospect of being back at Riversham alone was not at all enticing.

Rocky laughed. "You haven't lost your heart to the big city, then?"

Melinda shook her head. "No." Her heart was lost to a man.

"How did you manage to talk Kyle around?" Rocky asked as they got into the car.

Melinda was startled. "What do you mean?"

Rocky raised a surprised eyebrow. "You don't know? But we thought it must have been all your doing. Last night Kyle phoned Matthew. Quite late. It must have been after midnight over there."

Melinda held her breath. Kyle was a vivid presence in her mind. "And ... what did he say?"

"He's agreed that Matthew can stay. For a while, anyway. Until he reviews the whole Heronvale situation in six months' time. Mrs. Macintosh is delighted, of course. And your young fan is ecstatic."

Melinda felt weak with relief and gratitude, but skeptical that she'd had any influence on Kyle. Something must have changed his mind, but she didn't think it had been her. Well, perhaps some of the things she'd said had made him think. . . .

"This is wonderful news, Rocky," Melinda said. "I think Kyle is beginning to realize just how much of a rough time Matthew has been having since the divorce—and even before the breakup. He was so weighed down with his own misery after the divorce, and so inexperienced with children, he just let things ride and hoped they'd work themselves out. And after that bitter custody battle, he was so afraid of losing Matthew. He loves the boy but doesn't find it easy to show his affection."

Rocky nodded. "Kyle's a deep sort of guy, and can seem intimidating. No doubt he's often preoccupied and gives the kid short shrift. They'll probably get along a lot better if they're out of each other's hair at least for a while. It'll give them both time to straighten things out. Matthew's been on tenterhooks ever since he knew his father must have been back from overseas."

"Poor kid. It must have been torture for him. So, what happens now? Matthew will go up to Heronvale, I presume."

"Yes. Deb would have been happy for him to stay with us, but we don't really have enough room, and anyway we were afraid Mrs. Macintosh might have felt slighted." He glanced at her as they pulled away from the parking lot. "Maybe we'll see Kyle coming over more often now."

Melinda avoided his eyes. "Maybe."

When they drove out of Heronbush and onto the road to Riversham, the vineyards looked greener even than when she had left. Melinda felt a surge of pleasure, but deep down knew that she could leave it all now if Kyle wanted her. Ten years ago, at nineteen, she'd doubted her capacity to love a man more than her beloved valley. Now she knew that if she couldn't have both, she would choose the man.

"Dot's been in," Rocky said as they pulled up outside Riversham homestead. "You'll find everything spick-and-span, and plenty of food. I expect you'd like a chance to unwind, so I won't let Matthew come up to see you just yet. I'll be taking him to Heronvale this afternoon, so he can come before we go."

"It doesn't matter, Rocky. Let him come now if he wants to."

He was adamant. "No, he can wait."

Rocky carried her luggage into the house and after a short discussion about the need for a new cellarhand he departed. Melinda kicked off her shoes and made a pot of tea. She felt suddenly weary and stupidly emotional as she carried her cup into the family room and put her feet up on the cane lounger. Sydney seemed like a dream now. She closed her eyes wearily, trying not to think about it.

Melinda dozed for an hour or so, then woke, had something to eat and a shower, and felt better. Already it was beginning to seem she had not been away. She was just going down to say hello to Gianni when Matthew arrived.

He came in and perched on a stool at the kitchen counter while she made him an orange drink and opened the tin of biscuits Dot had made. *"Biscotto, signorino?"* she offered.

"Grazie, signorina!" he answered, taking one and grinning at her. "How was Sydney?" he inquired warily.

"Great. I was very impressed with your house. And the rest of Sydney. Your father took me sight-seeing."

Still wary, Matthew asked, "How is he?"

"He's fine."

There was a long pause and then, "I suppose he was very angry when he found out I'd run away?"

"A bit. It was a shock."

"Well, he says I can stay now. Thanks for talking him around, Melly."

"I'm not sure I can take the credit for it. He was already thinking about it. You could have ruined everything, you know, by running away. That might have made him dig his heels in. Luckily, it didn't."

"He said he might come over for Christmas," Matthew revealed.

Melinda's heart gave a lurch. "Oh, did he? Well, that'll be nice." She wasn't sure if the prospect gave her pleasure or pain.

"You can come to our place for Christmas dinner," Matthew invited. "And you can go to the Jacoviches for tea."

"Thank you. I sure like people to organize my life for me!" Since her father had died, Melinda had spent Christmas Day with Rocky and family. She wasn't sure Kyle would want her at Heronvale for Christmas dinner or that she would want to go. But there was no way to explain the problem to Matthew.

"Rocky says it's all right," Matthew assured her. "I'm going there for tea, too."

He went on excitedly to tell her that he had already started going to school in Heronbush with Robert and that Kyle had given his approval. "It's terrific," Matthew enthused. "Much better than my old one."

Looking at him, Melinda felt her heart breaking all over again. With his dark eyes and melting smile, Matthew was so like his father that she wondered how she was going to bear seeing him about the place from now on.

Melinda didn't want to go to the auction of Jarrahwood but neither could she stay away. It was to be held on the property and from what she had heard a good crowd was expected. A lot of people were interested in buying the acres. There would be a sprinkling of local vignerons, doubtless a few potential hobby farmers and maybe a few investors. There would be the usual crowd of sightseers, like herself, curious to see who it would be knocked down to and how much was paid.

There would be no one willing to buy it and preserve it, that much Melinda knew for certain. Finally she'd had to accept defeat. In the weeks leading up to

the auction she had tried every avenue to save Jarrahwood, without success. She had contacted environmental groups and shown people the area's attributes
but, although their experts acknowledged its unique-
ness and deplored its destruction, without finance—
which they didn't have—nothing could be done, as it
was private property. There were other much more
urgent and vital environmental issues to be tackled,
she was told. The best thing to do, they'd said, was to
raise support locally. Melinda knew there was no one
else in the valley who would want to fight for Jarrahwood's preservation. She would have made herself
look ridiculous if she had tried. Reluctantly she gave
in and resigned herself to the loss of Jarrahwood forever.

On the morning of the auction she was still dither-
ing about whether she'd go or not, but in the end she
succumbed to a masochistic desire to witness it going
under the hammer. It would be a harrowing experience seeing it sold, but she had to be there.

When she arrived there was already quite a crowd
gathered around the veranda of the old house. Melinda saw a few familiar faces and greeted people she
knew. She caught Mrs. Marchant's eye and lifted a
hand in acknowledgment and sympathy.

She was about to make her way over to her when the
auctioneer called for proceedings to commence. He
began his preamble and in a few minutes the bidding
began. Melinda felt a deepening sense of loss as the
price rose briskly with several people putting in bids,
but as it went higher, some dropped out. Jarrahwood
was not going to be sold at a bargain price. Local bidders gradually dropped out and those left looked to

Melinda more like agents for clients than the clients themselves. Maybe some rich hobby farmer had his eye on the property, she thought. All kinds of professional people were starting vineyards these days. Interest in wine making was booming. Their keenness to buy had been pushing up land prices for some years.

"It's gone over the reserve," someone near Melinda remarked.

Melinda saw the smiles on the faces of Mrs. Marchant's sons and wished she hadn't come. She couldn't stand any more. In a moment it would be knocked down to one of the two remaining bidders. Miserably she looked away from them across the crowd clustered around the veranda where the auctioneer's table had been set up, and suddenly caught her breath. On the far side of the crowd, head and shoulders above those around him, was a familiar but totally unexpected figure. Kyle!

Her heart gave a lurch. She'd had no intimation that he was coming to Heronvale—Christmas was still weeks away. She wondered what had brought him over now. Anxiety about Matthew, or maybe business in Perth? He was not looking in her direction, but talking to someone near him. Possibly he had not even spotted her yet, her small figure being easily hidden in the crowd. She was a little surprised that he had bothered to attend, but she supposed he might be as curious as the valley locals.

"And more bids . . . are there any more bids?" The auctioneer was looking intently around the crowd pressing close to the veranda. There was silence and Melinda swallowed hard. This was it. It was like being at an execution. He would bang the gavel down and cry "Sold!" and that would be the death knell for Jarrahwood. Emotion welled up in her and tears misted her eyes. She felt unable to face anyone right now, and especially Kyle.

With the auctioneer's call ringing in her ears she slipped away unobtrusively, skirting the old house and running down the track through the bush that would eventually bring her back to Riversham. Her mind felt numbed. Tears rolled down her cheeks as she stumbled along the rough path. At the creek crossing she stopped and rested her head against a tree, flinging her arms around it in a despairing gesture.

She crossed the creek on the stepping-stones and sank onto the log on the other side, engulfed in misery. How was she going to bear it when the bulldozers came in, when all day long she would hear their droning, the crashing of trees, and see the landscape altering? Where would the animals and birds go? They would flee along the heavily treed riverbanks, she supposed, perhaps for long distances until they found refuge. But the trees and the wildflowers could not flee. They would be crushed. The great gum trees would crash to the ground and be turned into logs or burned on the spot. The rest would be flattened, ploughed in and obliterated. All gone to make way for a few thousand vines. It was desecration, vandalism.

The tiny ground orchids, the delicate cowslips, enamel orchids, spider and donkey orchids, all would be gone, their roots wrenched from the soil, and no one would even know they were ever there. The wildflower season was over now, the plants dormant until next spring. For those in Jarrahwood, there would be no more springs.

Melinda stared at the ground, disturbing the leaf mold with a stick, watching ants and other small insects at work in their soon-to-be-destroyed world.

She wasn't aware of him until Kyle lowered his large frame onto the log beside her. She turned, startled, and met his searching gaze.

"I guessed I'd find you here."

"What are *you* doing here?" she asked, trying to level her voice. Seeing him unexpectedly like this on a day that was already emotionally charged was almost too much to bear. "Matthew didn't say you were coming."

He smiled. "He didn't know. I didn't know myself until yesterday."

"I saw you at the auction," she said.

"You sneaked off before it was over."

"I couldn't bear it." She stood quickly, unnerved by him, wishing he hadn't followed her. "I—I've got to go." She added, "I'm glad you decided to let Matthew stay for a while." She edged away, but he stood, too.

"Don't go yet, Melly. I want to talk to you."

He was beside her, holding her in his arms, eyes searching hers.

"Kyle, please let me go."

"I love you, Melly."

She shook her head. "No..."

"Yes. And this time I'm not going to ask you to leave the valley. *I'm coming back.*"

Melinda swayed in his arms, unable to believe. Yet his lips had formed the words, her ears had heard them. "You can't do that," she said weakly.

"I want to," he said.

"Not just for me," Melinda said shakily.

"Katherine says you love me."

"I never said..."

His lips brushed hers. "Do you, Melly?"

"Yes." It was a small sound, muffled by the fabric of his shirt where her head was buried.

He lifted her face and made her look at him. He was smiling. "Good. Now we can talk. Come and sit down."

Melinda felt as though she must be fantasizing. This was too illogical and improbable to be reality. Kyle coming back to the valley was as unlikely as snow at Christmas.

"I've been having a pretty bad time lately," he said, "which is mainly your fault."

"I'm sorry."

He held her in the crook of his encircling arm, her head against his shoulder. "I think I knew when I saw you at my father's funeral that I was going to fall in love with you again, but I didn't want to. My life was already complicated enough. But as the days went by, wanting you drove me crazy."

"Kyle, that's not enough...passion isn't love...."

"I know, and I tried to pretend to myself that all I felt was passion, that if I made love to you the obsession would fade. I didn't want to become involved, Melly. But the more I saw you, the more I realized what a selfish young fool I'd been ten years before. I was young and wanted the world. I loved you, but other things seemed more important. I was arrogant, as youth often is. I wanted to have my cake and eat it, too. I didn't think of your needs, only my own. When you refused to come with me, my vanity was hurt. I told myself you didn't love me after all, because if you'd choose the damned valley instead of me..."

Melinda looked up at him. "I was frightened, Kyle. The valley was my home, my security, and I was scared of the unknown. I was never adventurous like you, or Rose or Sylvana or Caroline or Katherine. I was happy here."

"And you still are, I know. You made it very clear you were dedicated to continuing in your father's footsteps, winning gold medals, putting Riversham on the map. I knew I had even less chance of weaning you away from the valley now."

Melinda shook her head slowly. "It isn't really like that, Kyle, not anymore. Ten years ago I was too young. I was afraid to cut my ties, too young to love properly. I wasn't sure enough of you, or myself. It's different now. I didn't recognize my real needs then, but now I know I'd go to the ends of the earth with you, Kyle, and so long as you loved me I'd be happy. I chose the valley once, but not now." She smiled reassuringly. "I mean it, Kyle. You don't have to come back for my sake. If you want me, I'll go wherever you go."

Kyle looked stunned. "But, Melly, Riversham is your life."

"No, it isn't. I've realized that life is very empty without love. People are more important than places."

He was raking his hair in amazement. "But you're a valley girl, your roots are here—surely more now than ever."

She shook her head. "That's what I thought, but it's not true. When you're very young your roots can be important because they're your security. It's the same when you're old, you need to cling to the familiar. That's why it's cruel to uproot people like your mother and Mrs. Marchant. But in between, love is more important than roots. Your mother put down new roots in a new country and I can do the same. I'll miss the valley, of course, but I won't let myself pine for it. I love the valley, Kyle, but it doesn't belong to me and I can't stop it changing. I tried, but I couldn't even prevent Jarrahwood being sold." She asked almost inaudibly, "Which one of the two bidders left got it?"

"Neither."

Melinda blinked. "Neither!"

"No. I outbid them, Melly."

She felt sure she must have heard him wrongly. "You mean *you* bought Jarrahwood?"

"Yes."

"Kyle, you're joking! Why would you do that?"

"Several reasons. One is that, as I told you, I'm coming back to Heronvale."

"You're deceiving yourself, Kyle. You'll soon want to escape again."

"No, it's different now for me, too. I'm ready to come home. I fought the idea tooth and nail at first. But I lost the battle, Melly. Between the two of you, you and Matthew showed me what I really wanted. All at once I found myself making some surprising decisions. I knew I had to let Matthew stay at Heronvale, and when I gave in to that, suddenly I realized I wanted to be there, too. I began making plans for the place. And I told myself that if I was back at Heronvale, I might still have a chance with you...."

"Oh, Kyle, I can't believe it," Melinda whispered. She clung to him. "I was so hurt when you married Gina so soon after you left the valley."

He held her tightly. "I was angry with you, my pride was hurt and I thought you didn't love me. Gina was beautiful and glamorous and gave me a ticket into the kind of life I hankered after. She was also Italian, which helped to placate Mama over my leaving. I married Gina on the rebound, Melly, and it was a disaster almost from the first day. I was never really in love with her, only with what she represented. In a way I married her to spite you. It was a kind of statement—I'm free, free of the valley. This is the kind of life, the kind of wife I want, this is my new world." He smiled regretfully. "I was so arrogant, but I was surely punished. You should feel sorry for Gina. I do."

Melinda let his warmth enclose her. Something wonderful was happening, but so fast she couldn't believe it yet. And suddenly she remembered what he had also just told her, that he'd actually bought Jarrahwood himself. Melinda caught her breath. "Kyle, why did you buy Jarrahwood? To plant it up with vines?" Kyle had never felt the same way as she had about it, and if he did intend coming back for good, naturally he'd want to extend Heronvale. Jarrahwood provided the perfect opportunity. She looked at him apprehensively, and he kissed the end of her nose.

"No, my love, I shall never desecrate your precious Jarrahwood. That's why I bought it. To stop anyone else from ever doing so." He reached into his pocket and withdrew a piece of paper. "Here you are, a little present from me."

"What is it?"

"The sale note for Jarrahwood."

"So?"

"Read it. It's in your name."

Melinda stared incredulously at the document. She blinked until it came into focus. Her name leaped out at her.

Kyle was saying, "Your name will be on the title deeds, Melly. Jarrahwood will belong to you, legally, unconditionally."

Melinda could scarcely take it in. "You bought it—for me?"

"I thought it might make a suitable wedding present."

"Kyle...?" Her mouth trembled and for some moments she couldn't find any words. At last she said, "I—I once toyed with the idea of asking you to lend me the money to buy Jarrahwood, but when we talked about it I didn't think there was a hope you'd finance me. If there had been, you'd have suggested it yourself. You just didn't see it as I did."

He slid his arm around her shoulders and drew her against him. "I do now. You taught me so much these past months, Melly. About myself, about Matthew, about you and about the valley. Unconsciously, you showed me things I'd never really noticed before, and reminded me of things I'd forgotten. I felt the changes happening even before I went back to Sydney. I resisted them, but I was powerless.

"And after you came to Sydney, I knew I'd reached a crossroads. That night after you left, I was sitting all alone looking at the harbor lights, and my longing was so great it was actual pain. Not physical longing, but something so much deeper. I kept remembering that day we picnicked by the river. You and Matthew and I, we were just like a family that day, and I'd never seen Matthew so happy—to tell the truth, I hadn't felt so happy myself in a long time. You brought Matthew and me closer than we'd ever been before. It had never been like that with Gina.

"That last night you were in Sydney I should have told you I loved you, but so many things were still making it hard to come to terms with—my failed marriage, the way I'd treated you before.... But when you'd gone, I knew nothing mattered but being with you. There was no choice to make anymore. I wanted to fly home with you the next day, but I was afraid you'd reject me. I didn't know how you really felt, if it really was only a physical thing with you. Then Katherine told me I must be blind if I couldn't see you were in love with me. But that wasn't enough." He paused, gazing at her for a moment. "I needed to prove to you that I really wanted to come back to the valley for good. I was desperate because there seemed no way.

"And then out of the blue I started thinking about Jarrahwood and I suddenly discovered that I wanted it preserved, too. It's a part of my heritage, too, and I want my kids to be close to nature, to run free in the bush, learn respect for the environment, the wildflowers, the birds and animals, as we did. I want to make sure they know the simple pleasures we knew as children. In this mad world, Melly, we more and more need even small wildernesses like Jarrahwood that so-called progress cannot touch, ever."

He was telling her that! "You remembered the auction date?" Melinda asked.

"No. I was frantic, thinking it might have already taken place. I phoned Mrs. Marchant yesterday, and she told me it was today. I just had time to catch a plane. I had to buy it, not just because I wanted to preserve it, but because I knew that would convince you that I really have come back for good."

Melinda fingered the piece of paper in her hand. "It's the most wonderful thing that has ever happened to me. I can't believe I deserve so much—you *and* Jarrahwood."

He lifted a tendril of hair from her forehead. "Melly, you deserve far better than me, but if you'll have me . . ."

"Kyle, are you sure this is what you want? I meant what I said about going with you."

He stroked her hair tenderly. "Melly, I know you meant it, but it isn't necessary. Besides, whatever you say, you are like the wildflowers, not easily transplantable. Maybe with a lot of tender loving care you would survive, but you belong here and here is where you'll be happiest. And so now will I."

"What about your business? What happens to the hotels?"

He held her hands tightly. "There'll be no problem about getting someone to take over my business, darling. I'll set things in motion just as soon as I can. I can't wait to get started on building up Heronvale again." He looked at her seriously. "I hope you'll still run Riversham, of course, but will you come and live at Heronvale? We'll build Mama and Rosa a nice modern cottage down by the river, which is what my mother would like. And of course Mrs. Marchant can stay in her house, which we will have renovated for her, for as long as she likes. I've already told her.''

"And Rocky will move into Riversham home-stead,'' recited Melinda, "and the new cellarhand will take over his house." At Kyle's slightly puzzled look, she said, "Oh, Matthew had it all worked out ages ago. He's a great organizer. I'm to have Christmas dinner with you and tea with the Jacoviches."

"In that case, they'll have to have me, too!" said Kyle, laughing. "I'll not be parted from you for a minute."

"I'm sure they'll be delighted."

He looked steadily into her face, his hands on her shoulders, trembling slightly, as she was. "Melly, does this mean you believe me?"

She fingered the piece of paper. "I think I have to now."

"And will you marry me?"

She nodded silently and her eyes filled with tears of happiness.

"Melly..." He threaded his fingers through her hair and drew her head close to his, whispering between kisses, "We've got a lot of catching up to do, so can we get married soon?"

Her eyes were sparkling. "A valley wedding?"

"Of course. Mama will insist. Before Christmas?"

"That's only a month away."

He said eagerly, "Plenty of time for banns, and to organize a good old-fashioned Italian wedding."

Melinda said anxiously, "Your mother, will she mind too much that I'm not Italian?"

He laughed. "She married a Scot herself. And she approved of you in the first place."

"We can be married in the old church and have the reception in the hall," Melinda mused. "Gianni can give me away, Matthew can be a page and maybe Katherine would fly over and be my attendant."

"We can have a honeymoon somewhere exotic and secluded and be back in time for the grape picking," Kyle added enthusiastically.

"I wonder what Matthew will say."

"He'll be over the moon." Kyle laughed. "Although I don't know how he'll react to dressing up as a page!"

Melinda clung to him and felt his warmth spread all through her. "*I'm* over the moon."

He ruffled her tousled red-gold hair. "So am I! I love you, Melly. So very much. And in the end that's all that matters, isn't it?"

"Yes, Kyle, it is."

He kissed her with tenderness, but passion quickly flared and deepened, and after a moment Kyle lifted his mouth from hers. "This is hardly the most comfortable place in which to show you how much I love you. Come on, let's go home."

*   *   *   *   *

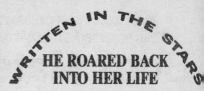